DANGEROUS

◆

INHERITANCE

Diane Winters

ISBN 978-1-63575-887-0 (Paperback)
ISBN 978-1-63575-888-7 (Digital)

Christian Faith Publishing, Inc.
296 Chestnut Street
Meadville, PA 16335
www.christianfaithpublishing.com

Printed in the United States of America

To Lennie and in memory of my parents

CHAPTER 1

"How did that saying go? The corn is as high as an elephant's eye on the fourth of July? Close enough." Maggie Chesney walked down the tree-lined lane, perspiration beading up on her forehead. The breeze was almost nonexistent, and if the trees hadn't provided a canopy of shade, there was no way she would be out walking in the middle of the afternoon in the month of June. The old farmhouse had one swamp cooler in the kitchen window, and it only worked half the time. As Maggie drew close to the barnyard, she turned and continued to walk under the cover of the trees, then stopped by an old elm tree where a swing was suspended by a rope. She absently moved it back and forth and then looked up at the branch it was tied to. The swing had been there so long the bark had grown over the rope. Maggie gave a brief smile as she looked around. The grass was burning from the heat and too little rain. She needed to buy new hoses and sprinklers if she was going to keep the grass alive. She sighed as she looked back over her shoulder to the barn. There was no money in the budget for repairs. Shoot. There wasn't a budget. Her father had died this last spring and left the old homestead in a sad state of repair.

When the will was read, she and her brother were given the old Nebraska farm equally. Robert immediately requested the lawyer to draw up the paperwork necessary to have Maggie handle the estate as the personal representative as she was going to be staying at the farm indefinitely and Robert was headed back to Chicago. Robert had all intentions of signing the farm over to Maggie when the estate was settled, so she went right home after saying good-bye to Robert and his family and decided to read the land leases. Not that she knew much about farming, but it didn't take a rocket scientist to realize her father was on the losing end of the lease. It was no wonder he never had any money. Maggie was just glad there wasn't a mortgage or debt at the bank. The life insurance policy her father had paid for the funeral and a few expenses with nothing left over to care for the house. Her brother and family stayed only long enough to hear the will and took off for home. As she looked around the roughened homestead, she didn't blame them at all.

Maggie was a twenty-eight-year-old schoolteacher by trade, and with her father's passing, she requested and was granted to be let out of her teaching contract. Maggie felt deep down in her core that she needed to return to her old home and try to keep it in the family. The homestead was settled by her great-grandfather and had been handed down to the next generation along with additional sections added as the years flew by. By the time it was handed to Maggie and Robert, there were a total of eight sections, and all of them were leased to some of the neighbors who had land adjoining theirs. Robert told her to sell it all off and get rid of the albatross, but she knew that wasn't the answer. Her mother had died on this homestead, having thought to have had a long bout of the flu, which turned out to be appendicitis instead. By the time she had agreed to go to the hospital, it was too late to save her. After her mother died, her father lost interest in life. They had married later in life and loved each other very much. He puttered around the farm for the next twenty-three years without actually doing much of anything. He managed to make enough money to keep everyone in clothes and for food, but without his wife beside him, he lost interest in making the farm successful. He did spend quality time with his children and managed to finish raising them on his own without too much trouble. His sister June would step in and help with Maggie when she needed a mother's touch or advice over the years. June had died from a massive heart attack a couple of years previously. It was difficult for Maggie as June was the only mother whom she could really remember. June had never married, so there were no more relatives living in the area. Her mother had been a foster child and never knew any of her own family. The Chesneys had developed strong relationships with the neighbors and enjoyed their life together. No, she couldn't sell. It just wasn't in her to let her childhood home be sold and no longer be held by the family.

Robert had left home at the ripe age of eighteen and never looked back. He didn't want anything to do with the farm that actually required physical labor. He loved to tinker and tear apart machines to see how they worked, and would attempt to find out why something had broken down. When a repairman came to work on something their father couldn't fix, Robert peered over their shoulder and asked a million questions. As a teenager, he repaired and worked on many a problem but had no desire to spend any time in the fields or learn about farming itself. Their father realized that Robert would never take over the farm, and as he aged, he gradually rented the farmland out to the neighbors and attempted to keep up the major repairs himself. Robert went on to become an electrical engineer and the thirty four year old was married with two children of his own now. Happy as could be, he was enjoying city life and rarely came home for a visit. He had taken a job after college with a large corporation on the outskirts of Chicago and had quickly climbed the corporate ladder. He met his wife through work and she was very happy to remain at home with the children and be the corporate wife for Robert. Maggie loved them all, but she knew that wasn't the life for her.

Maggie left the shade trees of the large yard and decided to walk to the pond. She passed the barn with its sagging roof and doors off the hinges, the granary that had stood empty for the last twenty-some years, and the empty chicken coop. The pond was about one hundred yards farther from the barnyard through tall grasses that were moving gently as she walked through them. She could hear the frogs croaking, becoming louder the closer she came to the pond. When she reached the edge, she was disappointed to see it was almost dried up. As she looked around at the dry cracked ground, she realized that over the years it had filled in with dirt and weeds. Maggie remembered when she and Robert were younger they would bring their friends down to the pond and jump in and swim around on the hot days of summer. They would catch tadpoles and frogs and try to put them down their friend's shirts. She chuckled as she remembered ice-skating in the winter while having a bonfire to warm up when needed, toast marshmallows, and have hot chocolate. Maggie had a terrible crush on a neighbor boy by the name of Joe, and she would invite him over for all their get-togethers at the pond. The problem was, he was always following Sheila around instead of her. Last she heard, they had gotten married and had several children. Maggie sighed. She turned and went back the way she came, anxious to get to the house for a tall glass of ice tea and hoped that the swamp cooler in the kitchen window was working. *Tomorrow is another day.*

Maggie walked into the house and looked around the kitchen. The appliances were serviceable, and there was even a microwave that still worked. She had brought home a few groceries, and as she put them away, she looked at the jars and bottles still in the refrigerator. She started a list of things she would need to attend to, and number one was cleaning out the refrigerator. Maggie poured a glass of ice tea and sat with her back to the swamp cooler and the ledgers in front of her. She had brought out her father's ledgers and file from his office as she couldn't bring herself to sit at his desk right now. As she cooled off and enjoyed her tea, she realized it was getting dark out and it was only four in the afternoon. She walked over to the window and noticed a large rain cloud forming to the west, and it had a green shade to it. *That doesn't look good. And it wasn't there a little bit ago when I was outside!* Maggie grabbed her keys to the car and decided to pull it into a shed with a door that actually closed. When she got out of the car, she looked up at the roof of the shed and noticed it still looked solid. She closed the shed door and hurried back to the house, looking at the storm forming quickly behind her. Growing up, she had seen plenty of storms and knew that this one was going to be nasty. When she got back to the house, she shut off the swamp cooler; grabbed the ledgers, files, and tea; fixed a quick sandwich, then walked downstairs to sit on a comfy old couch. *I might as well make myself at home down here for a while.*

When Maggie arrived for the funeral, instead of getting a hotel room like her brother, she had cleaned up her old room in the basement of the house and organized it for a long stay. She washed sheets and hung them on the clothesline to dry and aired out her old mattress. It was a struggle to get it out the door, but after a few hours in the hot sunlight, it smelled fresh once again. There was an old TV on a stand and shelves of books accessible for long sleepless nights. The couch was an addition Maggie and Robert added when they were teenagers. Their aunt bought a new couch and let the kids move the worn one into the basement. It had seen many a teen hanging out on it over the years. The old recliner had seen better days, and Maggie threw it out, along with several bags of trash and items that she no longer needed to keep.

Maggie pulled over a TV tray she had set up and placed the ledgers on it. She sat on the couch, daydreaming as she nibbled on her peanut-butter-and-jelly sandwich. As she finished up her sandwich, she could hear the wind picking up speed. She reached over to the stack of papers and noticed the leases were all exactly the same except for one. Maggie hadn't read them thoroughly before but studied them now by a reading light. The leases all said that if the crops failed, the person leasing the ground wouldn't owe her father a thing; otherwise, they would pay him one hundred dollars an acre after harvest was over. She picked up the one that had some added writing on the bottom. It was signed by their neighbor and friend Joe. He had made a notation that he would pay her father either way because he carried crop insurance. Maggie smiled. *Bless his heart. He knew that Dad was a pushover.* She picked up the other three leases and checked out the signatures. Maggie didn't know them except by name as her father had talked about them occasionally. She stacked them together and placed them to the side, then pulled the ledger to her. She stopped and listened to the rain, and the wind was starting to howl. She opened up the ledger to the first page and lovingly ran her fingers over the entries from years ago. Her father was meticulous in his bookwork and would spend hours making sure the entries were correct before moving on to the next month. As she flipped several pages over, she noticed one thing; the entries began to be less and less. She flipped several pages forward and looked at the date. Two years ago and there were only a couple of entries. Maggie turned the page. Nothing. As she skimmed through the rest of the book, she found no further entries. In stark realization, she knew that her father had been failing, but no one had noticed. But shouldn't she have noticed when she came to see him? He got around well and seemed to have a sharp mind when she visited. Why did he let the ledger go?

As Maggie sat there contemplating the business at hand, the storm moved from rain to hail. Maggie sat upright and listened to the pounding on the roof and the ground outside the window. She got up and walked over to move the curtain. All she saw were hailstones the size of baseballs and realized that there wouldn't be any crops this year, which meant no money for her to work on the house. And with hail that big, the roof was going to need repaired, for sure. Without the ledger being completed, Maggie wasn't even sure there was home insurance. She flipped the curtain back and walked back over to the couch. She flipped on the TV and turned it to the local channel. Sure enough, a storm warning was in effect for the next hour, but she saw no mention of a tornado warning. The wind was still blowing, but with the noise from the hail, it was difficult to tell how hard it was. Maggie grabbed her tea and settled in to watch TV until the storm subsided and would check everything out after it was over.

An hour later, the sun peeked out from the clouds, and Maggie realized it had stopped raining. She knew from the sound of the storm and looking out the basement window it wasn't going to be good news when she went outside. The hail lasted a long time, and she was concerned over what she would find. As she climbed the steps, she knew she better grab a jacket. She remembered how cold it could get after a storm of this magnitude. Maggie grabbed an old jean jacket on her way up the steps and walked out the back door. She stopped in her tracks. The hail was piled high against a barn that was no longer standing. The wind had knocked down the south side of the decrepit structure, and the whole thing was leaning over. Maggie sighed. *I guess I can leave fixing the barn off the list and put tearing down instead.* She shook her head as she looked across the barnyard. Water was running in little rivers everywhere and headed for the pond. Maggie reached inside the back door and retrieved some old overshoes and pulled them on. She slogged through the hail and up the lane again. As she stood looking at what was once a beautiful corn field, all she could see was ragged stalks and shredded leaves on the ground. Water and hail was standing everywhere. She would have to check who leased that property since there wouldn't be any income from it. Maggie looked across the fields and down the roads. She could see farmers in their pickups already driving around, scouting the damage. She walked back to the house and looked at the sagging barn once again. The shed her car was in appeared to be safe and dry. The old granaries were still standing, but she could see dents in the silos as she looked up and down the structures. Maggie turned and looked at the roof of the house. The shingles were shredded and large dents could be seen. She walked over to the west side of the house and noticed not one window was broken, but the tree leaves were shredded as they caught the hail before it hit the house. Behind the house, a large branch had split off a tree and just missed the roof by a few feet. Maggie went back inside and removed the overshoes. She walked upstairs and looked around for any leaks, but everything seemed warm and dry. She opened up a few windows to provide a cool breeze and sat down at the kitchen table. *I'm exhausted.* Maggie sat there for a few minutes more, wondering if she was as crazy as her brother seemed to think. *I'll look it over tomorrow. I just can't do anymore tonight.* Maggie got up and returned to the basement. As she got ready for bed, she realized that she was truly on her own. *I'm going to have to get some help.* Maggie turned in and shut the lights off, and in ten minutes, she was sound asleep.

The following morning, Maggie made a quick breakfast and ate it while looking out the kitchen window. The hail was still piled up against the buildings but was melting quickly as the air began to heat up. Water continued to run through the yard toward the pond. She could hear the frogs merrily croaking, happy to have water to play in again. The first thing she was going to do was throw away the list she had been making. It wasn't even close to covering the mess she had on her hands. After rinsing her dishes and putting them in the drain board to dry, she went back to her bedroom and looked for an old pair of boots. After digging them out of the back of her closet, she took them to the back porch and banged them around and shook them to chase away any spiders that might have thought her boots were the perfect hideaway. She slipped them on and went out to the shed and checked on her car. It was safe and dry, but she knew it wasn't going to drive well on the muddy roads after the downpour they had. Maggie walked over to another door and opened it wide. Her father's old Chevy pickup was sitting there collecting dust, but she knew it would run as her father had loved his truck and always took great care to make sure it stayed that way. It was the only thing he managed to keep running. She got in and turned the key, and the engine fired right up. Maggie smiled at the sound, then looked at the gas tank. She would have plenty of gas to get to town and back a couple of times. Maggie backed the truck out and drove it up to the house. She hopped out and went to retrieve her purse. As she slammed the back door tight, she realized that the back door was never locked. Even after her mother died, no one locked the door. Maggie thought about it and realized there was never was a lock. Living in the country, no one bothered. *Old habits die hard, but I'm going to have to get a lock.*

Maggie headed the old truck toward town. It was nine miles to Paxton, and all of it was going to be on country roads. That would give her time to look over the damage the storm may have caused to other areas. As she slid around the sloppy roads, she noted that several areas were almost washed away with the runoff from the storm. The ditches were full of water, and Maggie was certainly happy she thought to take the truck instead of her car, or she would have been sitting in a ditch within the first mile, drenched. Damage from the storm looked to be extensive. She didn't see a field that hadn't been damaged to some extent. Maggie rolled into Paxton and located her father's insurance agent. The sign on the door said *Closed. Great. I'll have to head on into North Platte to the main office.* The pickup was a comfortable ride and the engine smooth. Maggie made it to North Platte in another thirty minutes and found her way to the insurance office. As she opened the door, she could see several people sitting in the waiting room. This was going to be a long wait.

Maggie picked up a magazine and flipped through it as she sat down to wait. She looked around occasionally and noted how bored everyone looked. Turning to the person closest to her, she asked, "Been waiting long?"

The woman looked away from her book to Maggie. "About an hour. That evidently is the average time it takes to get anything done today. Everywhere I've gone it's been hurry up and wait."

Maggie smiled. "Well, then. I guess I better find a better magazine."

As she rifled through several types of magazines on the table, the lady next to her was called back into the office as someone left. After looking at almost every magazine on the table, Maggie began to look around her at the pictures and other customers. She got up and walked to the receptionist.

"You know, all I really want to know is if I have an active policy or not. Maybe you could help with that, or I can always come back another day."

"Have a seat, and let me look it up." The receptionist took her father's and Maggie's name and checked the computer for any policies under their names. She looked up at Maggie and responded, "It's your lucky day. The policy expires in two weeks, and your father had both you and your brother's name on it too. Do you want to take care of the renewal while you are here?"

"Yes. Let's get that taken care of today. You can take my dad's name off now that he is gone, but leave my brother's name on it." The receptionist nodded and began the paperwork renewal while Maggie grabbed her purse.

Maggie took out her checkbook and was in the process of filling out her check when she heard her name. "Maggie? Is that you?"

Maggie turned around and found her neighbor Joe and his wife, Sheila. "Well, I live and breathe! I was going to call you tonight!" Maggie jumped up and gave each of them a hug.

"We're sorry about your dad. It's got to be tough."

"Well, some days are harder than others, but I think I'm still in a bit of a shock over it. Let me finish up this check." Maggie signed her name and handed the receptionist the check, then turned to her friends. "Have you been in to see the agent yet, or are you waiting?"

"We stopped by to see them, but I can see they are backed up. We can come back later. Let's go get a cup of coffee or something."

"Be happy to. Just a second." She turned to the receptionist and told her she would return another day but to put her on the list for an adjuster to come to the farm. As she turned back to Joe and Sheila, they waved her on out the door. There was a coffee shop two doors down so they walked in and placed their orders.

After they settled into their booth, Joe looked up at Maggie. "Have you found the lease yet?"

"Yes, I did. I saw what you wrote on it. I appreciate your honesty."

"Your dad hasn't changed the price or terms in fifteen years. I kept telling him he needed to charge more over the years or change the terms, but he was satisfied with what he had, I guess."

Maggie sat holding her cup and looking out the window. Sheila reached over and took her other hand, and Maggie instantly got tears in her eyes. "The old coot just up and quit the last few years. Everything is a mess." Sheila continued to hold her hand but offered her a tissue. Maggie wiped her eyes and turned to look at the couple. "Come by the farm the next chance you get, and you will see what I mean. On top of everything else, the storm finished off the barn."

Joe nodded. "What are you going to do? Sell or what?"

"I don't want to sell. I just can't let it go. We can talk about leasing again, but I'm going to have to fix the current terms." Joe agreed and stated he would bring a copy of a lease he had with someone else that she could use to write a new lease for the future.

"Do you know any of these other men that leased from Dad?"

"Not really. I have my hands full, and we evidently don't run in the same circles. Why?"

"I just think that it's a raw deal that Dad dealt with them all this time but didn't insist on money up front or be covered when they collected their crop insurance. I know most of the time you get a crop, so the odds of storms like the one that happened yesterday are rare. But of all the years for it to happen! It leaves me with very little to operate on, and Dad didn't save much." Joe and Sheila commiserated with Maggie over the financial loss and said they would come and see her after their own adjuster was out. Maggie gave them both a hug before leaving them to return to the insurance office.

Maggie decided to drop on out to the big-box store and get some much-needed supplies. After picking out several hoses and sprinklers, she walked over to the air conditioners to see what they had. She found a small one that would be easy for her to install in the kitchen window and then figured she had spent enough money for the day. As she checked out, she grabbed a package of licorice to munch on while she drove home. After paying for her supplies and loading up the truck, she headed the truck for the farm. She stopped by McDonalds and got a sandwich and drink for lunch first. The licorice could wait until she finished her lunch. As she pulled into the driveway, she could see that things were beginning to dry up, and there was no longer water running through the yard, and the hail was completely melted. The humidity was high from all the moisture, and the heat was almost unbearable. As she stuck another piece of licorice in her mouth, she got out and grabbed the hoses and sprinklers from the truck bed and took them up to the house by the hydrant. Before grabbing the air conditioner, she reached into the truck to grab the licorice and her purse. She stuck another piece in her mouth and the rest in her purse, slammed the truck door, and grabbed the air conditioner. She trudged into the house and sat it on the back porch. *I can wait until tomorrow to install that thing.*

Maggie went up the steps and reached over to turn on the swamp cooler. Nothing happened. She messed with the knob, shutting it off and on, but it still didn't kick in. She checked the plug, then walked down to the fuse box. Everything was fine there. *Great. Either I sweat to death in this humidity, or I put the AC in.* Maggie went back to the kitchen windows and opened them up. She then reached over to the one with the swamp cooler in it, unplugged it, removed the window wedge, and pushed up the top part of window. She gave the cooler a little shove, and it fell out backward below to the sidewalk. The sound was deafening, but there wasn't anyone around to hear it anyway. With a satisfied clap of her hands, Maggie went to the back porch and opened the box with her new AC unit. She brought it up and sat it in the window and locked the window down with the wedge, just like the swamp cooler. It fit perfectly. She arranged the corrugated wings on the side and plugged it in. With a quick flip of the switch, it quietly began humming and cooling. Maggie went back to the box and found the little remote control that it came with and made sure there wasn't anything else in the box before pitching it outside.

Maggie went back up to the kitchen and poured herself another glass of tea. She sat thinking of her conversation with Joe and Sheila. She was going to like having them as neighbors, and she could trust them to help if needed. Speaking of help, she was going to have to put an ad in the paper for some part-time help. There was no way she was going to be able to manage all this mess without someone else to help her. Maggie looked at the clock and realized it was still early enough to call the paper office to place an ad to run for a couple of days in next week's paper. *I should have done this while I was in North Platte.* Maggie dialed the paper and placed an ad then decided to make a flyer to put up at local businesses. As she was scribbling out ideas on scratch paper, she heard a truck drive into the yard. She looked out the window and saw two men in a pickup had stopped in front of the barn, and it looked like they were studying it. Maggie went to the back porch and watched the men as they backed up and drove up to the house. The driver got out and came up to the house. The driver was tall and lanky and wore a neatly trimmed long beard. The one in the truck looked to be a teenager. Maggie went out to meet him.

"Excuse me, ma'am, but what are you going to do with the barn?"

"What do you mean what am I going to do with it?"

"Well, are you going to tear it down or rebuild?"

Maggie looked at him with a questioning look on her face. "Why do you ask?"

"Let me introduce myself. I'm Seth Johanssen, and that is my son, Mark. We live southwest of here about seven miles. I am looking for projects for our young men to provide assistance to others so they may learn to serve. I saw the barn from the road and thought that, either way, tearing it down or putting it back up would be a good service project for them."

Maggie crossed her arms and looked over at the barn. "You mean for free, or I pay them to do it?"

"I mean for free. As I said, it would be a service project."

"Let me get some boots on, and we can go take a look at it. I haven't had a chance to look at it up close since it collapsed, and you can help me determine if it's worth saving or not."

Mr. Johanssen nodded and walked to his truck while Maggie grabbed her boots. Seth and Mark stood looking at the barn while waiting for Maggie to arrive. Once she caught up with them, they walked around to the south side and looked at the caved in wall. Seth looked under the walls that had collapsed on it and stood back up.

"I'm sorry, miss, but the beams have all cracked under the pressure. You would need a new barn, but you don't have to take my word for it. You can get another opinion."

Maggie walked under the safest part of the roof and allowed her eyes to adjust to the dimness. She could see the struts and beams were cracked and toppled on top of each other. "I believe you are right, Mr. Johanssen. It needs a teardown. It was in bad shape before the storm. I hadn't been in it yet, but from the looks of it, I was probably safer to stay out here. So you have people willing to do this?"

"Yes, of course. And we will haul it all off. We can recycle some parts of it. Maybe we could rebuild something in its place such as a garden shed from the good lumber."

Maggie reached out to shake his hand. "I will allow you to bring your team over anytime to take care of it. We can talk about another structure once you start to tear this thing down. There might not be anything left that hasn't been termite infested."

"I appreciate you allowing us to serve you. Thank you, miss."

"It's Maggie. Maggie Chesney. I appreciate this so much. My father passed away and left this place to my brother and me. I need to work on a lot of things, and after the storm, it was almost too much to think about doing something with the barn."

"I'm sorry for your loss. We will be back soon. Do you need notice, or are there any bad times to work?"

"Nope, just come when you want and work as you can. I'll be delighted to have it torn down, and thank you so much for stopping by, Mr. Johanssen."

"Please call me Seth, and we will see you soon." The men got back in the truck and waved as they drove out of the yard. Maggie watched them leave and felt some relief fall off her shoulders. She made her way back to the house and was pleasantly surprised at how cool her kitchen felt. It was a good day after all.

CHAPTER 2

Maggie decided she had had enough excitement for the day and turned in early once again. She was sleeping well in her old bed, which surprised her. The quietness of the farm was always pleasant to her, and she relaxed once again, hearing the sounds of the distant frogs and crickets chirping. Before long, the sun was shining in her eyes once again. Maggie stretched and kicked the sheets off. She puttered around and fixed a bowl of cereal and stood at the window once again. The sight of the barn was depressing, so she changed windows. The yard looked great since the rain and had greened back up once again. She surmised it would be easier to keep it watered now. Once Maggie dressed, she remembered there was a rain gauge out on a fence post. She threw her boots on to go check and found it shattered from the hail. *Just one more thing to replace.*

Maggie walked through the yard and picked up a few branches. When she realized that it was going to be a big job to clean up the debris, she walked out to the old granary they used to store the mower. The cart was sitting there with flat tires. *Great.* She plugged in the compressor, and gratefully, it still worked. She waited as it built up pressure, then found she was able to pump the tires up with little difficulty. Maggie checked the mower tires while she was at it and found a gas can. After checking the oil level and noting the black color, she mentally added changing the oil to her never-ending list. *I might have to restart that list again.* She chuckled. The mower started up, and she hooked up the cart. She drove around the yard and picked up branches and debris until her cart was full. Maggie drove it to an old tree pile that was down away from the barnyard, dumped it, and went back to the yard to refill it. She even got the old swamp cooler picked up. The yard was six acres of grass and trees, and with that latest storm and ones that had previously hit without her dad picking up afterward, there was more trash than she could imagine. She needed to get it all picked up before she attempted to mow.

Maggie eventually stopped for lunch. She washed up and stretched her tired muscles. As she looked in the refrigerator for something to eat and was undecided on what to fix, she spied her licorice on the counter. She grabbed a piece and then went to her room to put her long black hair in a ponytail. Maggie found a baseball cap and threw it on. As she went back to the kitchen, she decided to fix another sandwich and have licorice for dessert. That and two glasses of ice tea, she felt ready to go back to work. Maggie snapped her fingers. *I need one more thing.* Maggie went back to her room and found her iPod and put in her earbuds. Once she was tuned into her music, she felt ready to spend the afternoon in the yard. She danced a bit on her way out the door and smiled as she realized she had accomplished quite a bit that morning. *One step at a time, girlie. One step at a time.*

As suppertime neared, Maggie realized how hungry she was. She unloaded the cart one more time and put everything away. The battery on her iPod had given out hours ago. Maggie decided to take a quick shower before finding something for supper. As she sat down to a mug of soup and crackers, she thought she should check her phone for messages. Maggie realized she hadn't even looked at it for a couple of days. As she ate, Maggie scanned the messages and looked at her Facebook page. She replied to messages and then checked her e-mail. There was nothing she needed to worry over today. She looked at the front of her phone and realized it was Saturday. *I better walk out to the mailbox and see if there is anything new in there since Tuesday. There will probably be more sympathy cards.* On her mental list of things were to buy thank-you cards too. *I better start that new list.* Maggie finished up her supper and rinsed her dishes. She walked through the yard to the road as the lane was still muddy from the storm. She inspected her cleanup work of the yard as she walked and realized she didn't miss too much debris. Maggie crossed the road and opened up the mailbox. There were stacks of mail, a paper, and a couple of magazines. *Good grief. I better check this more often, and I haven't even started to get my mail here yet.*

When she got back to the house, she threw everything on the table and reached over and grabbed another licorice. She thumbed through the mail and tossed aside the magazines and newspaper to glance at later. Maggie noted that much of the mail was junk and solicitations plus a couple of sympathy cards, but one caught her eye. It had the courthouse as the return address. Maggie grabbed the letter opener and slit the envelope. The letter she pulled out had her sitting down quickly. *No. It can't be.* Maggie continued to read, and it caused her to become more anxious the longer she looked at it. *How can this be?* Maggie threw it down on the table and went to her father's desk to dig in his files. She found unopened bills by the handfuls all dated in the last six months. Maggie brought them all to the table and began opening them one by one and putting them in separate piles. When she was done, she grabbed her phone and brought up the calculator. By the time she had finished adding it all up, she was officially in panic mode. Maggie felt the tears well up in her eyes and attempted to stifle a sob. *I don't have enough money for this, Dad! What were you thinking?*

The letter from the courthouse explained that the farm was delinquent in taxes and someone had paid them up for the last three years. If she couldn't come up with the money and pay the taxes herself, she could lose everything to a stranger. Then to top it off, her father had quit paying for most of his bills, and there were outstanding debts that totaled to more than ten thousand dollars. She was surprised to find the electricity still on after opening all those bills. The taxes alone would bankrupt her and Robert. Maggie sat in shock for another half an hour before shaking herself. She absently got up and reached for another licorice to chew on while she contemplated her dilemma. *Monday I'm going to have to see the banker. I hope they don't have any more surprises for me!* Maggie went back to the desk and looked around for more bills and the bank statements. The statements agreed with what the lawyer had set up for her, so that was a plus, but by the time she had paid the funeral expenses and the lawyer, she only had about five thousand left of her father's money. *I've got to find a job soon. Between the hail knocking out the lease income and these bills, this is going to be ugly.*

Maggie sat back down at the table and continued to nibble on licorice as she made a list of who needed to be paid. On another paper, she began the list of things she needed to repair. Maggie had her own savings, but she was hoping to leave it alone. She had already spent her own money on the new AC and hoses. As she thought about the needed repairs on the house from the hailstorm, she went back to the files, found a copy of the home insurance policy, and sat back at the table to read it over. It didn't cover the barn, but there was full coverage on the house. She felt relieved by that until she realized there was a five-thousand-dollar deductible. Maggie sat back. *Five-thousand-dollar deductible? No wonder the insurance was cheaper than I expected when I paid it up again.* Things continued to take a turn for the worse. Maggie threw her hands up, grabbed the rest of the bag of licorice, shut off the lights, and went downstairs to her room to eat licorice and feel sorry for herself.

Maggie contemplated calling her brother but knew he would just tell her to sell the place, not caring that she felt so much at home. As the truth smacked her directly in the face, Maggie realized that was just what she was going to have to do. She knew that the price of land was very good right now, and she would be set for life if she sold. There was no way she could let it go to someone for taxes and contemplated selling enough to pay the bills. As she looked around the dark and musty basement, the thought of letting it all go broke her heart. *Dad, I don't know what happened, but I'm pretty sure you didn't mean to leave me with this mess. I can't believe I didn't notice you were giving up. I don't know what to do, Dad. I don't even know who to call about all of this.* As Maggie prepared for bed, she threw what was left of the licorice on the dresser and crawled under the sheets. The evening had cooled off some, but the humidity was still high. She sighed and looked up at the ceiling and followed a spider crawling toward the corner of her room. As it made its way back and forth and formed a web, Maggie watched and began to relax. She decided to leave the spider alone and turned off the light.

When Maggie woke up, she felt groggy, and her muscles were screaming from all of her work in the yard and the tension that followed trying to understand her father's bills. After a bowl of cereal and some toast, she began to wake up. She reached over to her purse and pulled out her ibuprofen and took a couple of pills. *I should have taken some last night before I went to bed*, she surmised. Maggie walked around the kitchen, stretching her sore muscles. As she looked at the clock, she realized she would have plenty of time to make it to church. *Maybe I can find someone I can talk to that could help me make some decisions.* Maggie went back to the bedroom and threw on some light summer clothing and tied her hair back. She chose to not wear makeup due to the heat and her already tanned skin. Maggie backed her car out of the shed and drove into Paxton to the local Methodist church. She managed to make it on time and was able to visit with a few friends of her father's and thank the ladies for the dinner after the funeral before the service started.

Maggie chose to sit in a different pew than her father would have. She wanted to sit farther to the back so she could observe who attended and see if she knew anyone her age. Although she had attended church there all her life, she still felt out of place. As she began to look at the bulletin and reach for a hymnal, someone sat next to her and began to reach for the same hymnal. Startled, Maggie looked up at the person sitting next to her and hanging on to the same book. "Excuse me," Maggie said. She let go of the hymnal and reached over farther and picked up a different one.

"No, excuse me. I just usually grab this one every Sunday. You know, same pew, same Bible, same hymnal." Maggie smiled.

"Yes, I know. But I broke the rules today and sat in a different pew." They both chuckled as the service started. Maggie was quite aware of the man sitting next to her. There was no ring on his finger and no person sitting with him. He was the type of man that any girl would call tall, dark, and handsome; and Maggie was intrigued by his good looks, but some warning niggled in the back of her brain. She had never seen him before and knew he had to be new to the area. Occasionally, she would look to her side and could see he was staring at her. It caused shivers to run up her spine. Maggie tried to concentrate on the sermon instead of letting her mind drift to the problems waiting for her at home and the man sitting next to her.

The service concluded, and everyone made their way out of the building. The gentleman who had been sitting next to her had stopped as she began walking to her car and called out to her. "Excuse me. I thought I should introduce myself. I'm Gary Johnson. And you are?"

Maggie took the proffered hand and managed a light shake. His hand was as smooth as hers was rough. "I'm sorry. I should have introduced myself. I'm Maggie Chesney."

"Ah. I'm sorry for your loss. That was your father that passed away recently?"

"Yes, it was, and thank you."

"If I might, could I interest you in lunch to get to know you better?"

Maggie looked at the gentleman and continued to feel a bit uneasy about him. "I'm sorry. I really don't know anything about you."

Gary looked a little crestfallen. "I understand. Look. I'm a land agent. I buy and sell land in the area, and I'm perfectly safe. You can ask the minister." Gary smiled at Maggie, but she thought the smile was a little forced, and the warning alarms went off in her head once again.

"Not today, thank you, Gary. Maybe some other time."

"Do you plan to be around here for a while, or are you going back home?"

Maggie tried to stand a little taller than her five-foot-six-inch frame. "I am going home, so if you will excuse me?" Maggie turned her back and found her car without difficulty as she thought of his comment about her leaving. She thought he knew way too much about her business. Gary stood there watching her get in the car and leave. As he walked slowly to his own car, he knew his plan would come together one way or the other. Gary smiled broadly as he left the parking lot, waved at the remaining parishioners, and went to his own home. Maggie stopped by the local gas station and café and asked to place a flyer for part-time help. They both agreed and said if they thought of someone they would let her know.

During the rest of the day, Maggie thought back to the morning at church and meeting Gary. She didn't know if she imagined it or not, but felt she needed to listen to her gut instinct about the man. She thought she would ask around about him sometime when she went back to town. Maggie settled down at the table in front of her bills and pulled up an accounting program on her laptop. She worked for several hours to bring everything she knew about the farm's needs up to date so she could present it to the banker. Maggie hoped she would be able to meet with the banker right away on Monday. She glanced down at the time on the computer and realized it was getting close to suppertime, but again, the skies were darkening. The heat was unbearable, so she wasn't surprised to find another storm brewing. She grabbed her keys and put the car back in the shed. She shut the door behind her and then walked over and shut the door on the pickup for safe measure. She decided to walk toward the pond as it gave her a better view of the clouds. She stood looking up at the menacing dark clouds swirling above her and noticed the green tinge. *Good grief. We're going to get hail again.* Then she noticed a tail forming and dropping to the ground.

Maggie turned and ran back to the house. She gathered all of the paperwork she had been working on and stuffed it all in a file, gathered up her phone and laptop, and scooted downstairs. When she was growing up, tornados had come close to the house but had only taken a couple of trees and removed a roof off an old outbuilding. The house had never sustained any real damage, but they had always flown down into the basement and stayed on the west wall away from everything. After Maggie got to the basement, she decided to grab a pillow and blanket and placed her items beside her. She casually began to thumb through the file and reorganized the papers as she waited the storm out. Then she heard what sounded like a freight train. Maggie slammed the files together, grabbed her laptop and phone, turned the couch over, and crawled under it. Her pillow and blanket were jammed under there with her, and Maggie realized she was shaking.

The noise became unbearable as she laid there, her laptop under her cutting into her ribs. The house began to shake, and Maggie let out a scream. Then it was over, and the noise was gone almost as quickly as it began. She heard wind, rain, and hail briefly; and then it was quiet. Maggie tried to push the couch off her, but couldn't. As she tried to crawl out from under it, she realized that one of the bookcases had tipped over on the couch. She pushed several books away and managed to wiggle out from the couch and bookcase, over books and other items lying on the floor. She lay on her back and looked up. *Well, at least I don't see blue sky from here.* Maggie caught her breath and got up. She pushed the bookcase back along the wall and flipped the couch back over. Maggie grabbed the file and laptop along with her phone and threw it all on the couch. She turned and looked up the steps. Everything appeared to be okay, but she knew to be careful. As she climbed the creaking steps, she could hear the noises of the outside much clearer than she should have.

Once she got to the back porch, she realized there wasn't a back porch any longer. The whole side of the house was exposed. Maggie carefully picked her way outside and stood in the yard looking at the house and then around the whole place. She could follow the path that the tornado took. There were uprooted trees, the chicken house was smashed to bits, the house was next, and it took the back porch; then it went on through the rest of the yard, tearing up trees along the way. It missed the windmill, but the weather vane was gone. Maggie continued to stand there and stare at the house. The tears began to silently stream down her face. She was alone and at a loss of what to do. All the work she had done yesterday was completely undone and was a million times worse. This was going to require a tree trimmer and construction workers for the house. The bank was never going to loan her the money she needed to fix this mess, and she doubted her home insurance was replacement cost. She had quit reading the policy after she noted the deductible amount. She didn't even know if the house was stable enough for her to be in it. She stood there staring for a long time and finally became aware of someone driving into the yard. Maggie glanced over as the visitor stopped the truck in front of a large tree crossing her driveway. *Great. I can't even get out of here now.* She swiped the tears from her face.

A man got out of a beat-up pickup and worked his way around the tree. As he came closer, Maggie noted the work clothes and unruly hair. When he walked close enough to talk without yelling, Maggie cautiously questioned, "May I help you with something?"

"I'm Luke Johanssen." He extended his hand and smiled.

Maggie took the hand and felt the calluses of a working man. "Well, Luke, what can I do for you?"

Still smiling, Luke let go of Maggie's hand and stuck his hand in his pocket. "I saw the flyer at the gas station that you were looking for a little help, and when I saw the storm come through this area, I decided to run out here instead of call. And it's probably a good thing I did, because the lines are down for several miles." Maggie looked around and pointed to the house.

"It might be a little too late for some small repair jobs." Luke turned around and saw the exposed ribs of the house. When he turned back, he gave Maggie a small smile again.

"You're right. Things are a little beyond some small repairs. But you're all right? You didn't get hurt?"

"No. I was a good girl and hid in the basement." She realized how silly it sounded and chuckled. She looked at Luke with a puzzled frown. "Are you related to Seth Johanssen?"

Luke stopped smiling. "Yes, he is my father. Why?"

"He stopped by the other day and was going to bring a crew to get rid of the old barn." Maggie pointed over her shoulder. Luke looked to the area she was pointing and saw where a barn used to be and saw only a concrete slab and some footings. Maggie shrugged. "I guess he won't have to worry about it now."

"No, he won't, but we need to do something with the house, don't we?"

Maggie shrugged again. "I'm about ready to give up. This is almost too much for me now." Luke looked over at the house, and when he glanced back, he noticed the tears sliding down Maggie's cheeks once again. He cleared his throat.

"Look. My father and I haven't gotten along too well the last few years, but since he was already here about the barn, I'm sure they would work on the house instead. One thing my father and his group can do is build." Maggie looked over at Luke.

"What about you? Are you still interested in helping out? I can't afford much."

"I can help, but I need to stay out of my father's way so we don't argue. Let me give you my number, and you think about it for a few days. Then get back to me either way. I have my own business doing repairs and such, and I keep pretty busy, but I always have some slack times where I could use a few extra dollars." Luke gave Maggie his business card.

"'Repairs by Luke,' that's simple enough to remember. Listen. I need to see the banker. And now that I have this mess on my hands, I really need to see him. Once I find out where I stand, I can give you a call."

"That's fine. I hope to hear from you soon, and I'll even call my father and let him know what happened here. I'm sure he will send someone over to help with the trees and see about working on the house."

"Are you sure you want to call him?"

"It's okay. We don't hate each other. Maybe we're too much alike to be in the same room together." Maggie chuckled.

"Thanks. I appreciate it more than you know." Luke walked back to the truck and backed down the lane. He waved as he left. Maggie turned and looked back at the house. She had no choice in the matter. She couldn't leave with the trees down, so she would have to buck up and sleep with a hole in the house. Maggie turned to look at the shop with her car in it. There was a large tree in front of the building, but it had missed the roof. That settled it. She couldn't even get her car out to try and leave.

Maggie carefully walked back into the house and up the stairs. There was no electricity, but the kitchen looked intact. She was going to have to throw out food starting tomorrow, so she decided she would cook up whatever she could for supper and drink the milk. Maggie chuckled as she remembered she was going to clean out the refrigerator. There wasn't any choice, now. The floors felt solid as she walked around, but she didn't want to cause any further movement, so she remained as quiet as possible. Maggie walked downstairs to get her phone and noticed it was almost dead. She took it down to the shed and went in the side door to get to her car. She was able to slide open the big door before getting into her car and plugging her phone in. She watched it charge as she thought about the way things were developing. *God, are you telling me to sell and get out? How much more can I take?* Maggie looked around the old building and saw a trunk over in a corner covered with some old floor mats. She decided to kill time by looking at what was in the trunk. It was getting dark pretty quickly due to the hour, but she managed to move several items and then get the top of the trunk cleared off to take a look at inside. It wasn't until she was filthy with dirt that she realized the trunk was locked. *Great. I should have checked that out first.* Maggie went back to the car and noticed the phone was all but charged. She shut the key off, unplugged the phone, and trudged back up to the house. "I better call Robert and let him know about the place before he hears it on the news." Maggie propped herself on a floor beam from the porch before hitting Robert's number. She just knew this wasn't going to go well.

Of course, Robert was happy she was fine, but he told her repeatedly to sell the place and get out from under it. She explained about the financial mess she kept finding too. "Go back to your old job. Find a new one. I don't care, but get rid of that place. From the sounds of it, Dad left a mess behind. It's not your responsibility to fix it all up. If he didn't care enough while he was alive, I don't know why you care now that he's gone."

Maggie sighed. "I don't know, Robert. You never cared for the place like me. And I don't know why I am so attached to it. It's not like I remember Mom or anything. It's just . . . I don't know. Peaceful. I'm happy here. I know you don't understand that, but I just felt right coming back, but these last couple of days have really tried my patience, what with finding all those unpaid bills and someone trying to get the place for the back taxes. That, by the way, has my hackles up fierce. How dare someone take this land from all of us for ten cents on the dollar?"

Robert listened quietly as Maggie carried on. "You know, that doesn't seem right, does it? Listen, let me do some checking into that. You have your hands full right now, and you can't even get out of the yard. Let me know when you talk to the bank. If there is anything I can help with, let me know." Maggie was surprised by Robert's willingness to do anything, but she quickly recovered.

"Thanks, Robert. I could use some help. And that is an understatement. I'll send you pictures tomorrow. I never even thought about taking any before the sun went down."

"Sis, I love you. You're right, I never fit in there, but you always loved the place. I'll do what I can from here, but if it's too much, just sell it, take the money, and run!" They both talked about Robert's family and the Johanssens' offering to come over to help clean up the farm. Just before they hung up, Maggie remembered one more thing.

"Oh, and Robert? One more thing. I met a guy at church today that seemed to be a little, I don't know, shady or something. His name was Gary Johnson. He tried to get me to go to lunch with him, and I have no idea who he is, but it just felt wrong. He said he was in land sales or something. I didn't listen real close, because he kinda freaked me out. Something just doesn't feel right about his attention. Almost slick."

"Hmm. I'll do some checking on him while I'm at it. Listen, sis, I gotta run. Talk to you soon." They hung up. Maggie stood up and stretched. The call had gone better than planned once Robert had said his peace about selling the place. She was going to appreciate his help in whatever capacity he offered. She picked her way carefully into the house. She looked back out into the darkness and wondered if any skunks or other critters would try to come in. She decided she would shut the bedroom door for the night even though it would be stuffy. Maggie hadn't tried to open her window in years and knew it would be stuck shut. She dropped into bed that night and mentally reviewed her checklist in her head. It was getting longer every day.

CHAPTER 3

Maggie got up the next morning and opened her bedroom door carefully and peeked out. She didn't see any animals around and decided to make enough noise that if one was upstairs it would run scared. She did the best she could to get cleaned up for the day. Without electricity and water, it was a futile attempt. The humidity was high most of the night, and she stuck to her sheets. Maggie grabbed her laptop, phone, and her ever-growing file, and took them upstairs. From there, she worked to get a chair and a small table outside, along with a TV tray. She set up a makeshift desk, and on her tray, she placed a breakfast consisting of a bagel and the last of her now warm iced tea. As she nibbled on her bagel, she looked around the yard. The shade tree she was under was a huge elm, but it had lost several branches to the storm. There were several trees uprooted on the tornado's route, so she stayed clear of those areas. As she finished up her meager breakfast, she began making phone calls.

The first call went to her father's bank. When the receptionist answered, she asked to talk to and/or make an appointment with whomever her father had done business with lately. The receptionist paused a moment. "I believe it might have been William Jensen, but I will check and have him call you back. Would that be all right?"

"Yes, that would be great."

"Can I tell him what it is regarding?"

"Sure. Let him know I've sustained a lot of damage at the farm and would like to visit about some additional funding."

"Yes, ma'am. I will let him know as soon as he comes in." Maggie gave her the cell number and hung up. The next call was to the insurance agent's office. She visited with the same woman who had taken her check the week before. After telling her about the damage to the house and requesting the adjuster as soon as possible, she went on to her next project. Maggie proceeded to call everyone in her file of delinquent bills and explained about her father dying and would they please give her until the end of July to take care of business? Most of the businesses had heard about her father, and she only talked to a couple of them who were angry at having to wait. Those two threatened to turn the bills over to the creditor anyway, so Maggie agreed to send them a check later in the week. She explained that she was unable to get out of her yard to do any business until the trees were removed. Finally, after much discussion, both of the companies agreed to give her a little more time to get the bills paid. Thankfully, the bills weren't some of the bigger ones, and she was hoping to get many of the smaller bills paid soon.

Maggie had spent the better part of two hours working out solutions with the bills on her accounting program and finally had to quit when the battery died. She stood up and decided to go for a walk to stretch out her sore muscles. The yard was a complete disaster. Now that the barn and the chicken house were gone, she had a greater view of the countryside. She could see that the electric company was already out working in the neighborhood, which gave her great hope, but that didn't mean they would allow her to have electricity to the house in the shape it was in. As she looked out to the torn-up fields, she remembered that she had one more call to make. Maggie strode back to her makeshift desk and found the number for the courthouse. Once she was connected to the treasurer, Maggie explained about her father passing away and getting the notice in the mail. The treasurer was polite but firm about the taxes needing to be paid, and if someone else was willing to pay them, she was just fine with the whole matter. Maggie double-checked on how soon she would have to come up with the money and found she had until the end of August. She hoped the banker would come through and provide enough funding to cover the past due bills, repairs, and the overdue taxes.

It was turning off hot again, and the humidity was thick. Maggie moved her table and chairs to stay in the shade of the big elm tree as the day wore on. She knew it wouldn't be any cooler in the house, and at least she had something besides the four walls to look at. Maggie seemed to be living on peanut butter sandwiches, but it was about all she could tolerate in the heat. She wandered down to her room in the basement and found what was left of the licorice and brought it back outside with her. She no sooner took a bite of peanut butter when her phone rang. She choked a bit trying to get it swallowed before answering her phone. It was the bank, and she didn't want them to hang up.

Maggie sounded a bit strangled when she answered. There was a pause before the banker replied. "Hello? Are you all right? This is Mr. Jensen from the bank." Maggie had managed to swallow her bite of sandwich, but she didn't have anything left to wash it down with.

After a quick cough, Maggie replied, "Yes, I'm sorry, Mr. Jensen. I was eating something and choked a bit. I'm fine now. Thank you for returning my call."

"No problem. I understand you would like to see me about some funds. And I hear you were hit with the storm yesterday. Is it bad?"

"Well, my house is standing except for the back porch, but when I lost that, it put a big gaping hole in the side. I have trees down all over, and I can't get out of the yard yet. I'm waiting for someone to come and clear them for me."

"I see. So what are you needing funds for these days? Your father has been leasing out the land for several years."

"I have a list of bills he had failed to pay in the last several months, and I also found out he hadn't paid the land taxes for three years, and someone else has caught them up. If I plan to keep the place, I need to get those paid shortly. I'm waiting for the adjuster on the house, but the deductible is five thousand dollars. As you can see, I'm in a little bit of a bind. I would e-mail the list to you, but I don't have any services of any kind right now."

"Well, that does put you in a bind. I tell you what. The least I can do is make sure you don't bounce a check, so I can put a notice to pay any check that you write for now as long as you don't go over one hundred dollars. When do you think you can get out of the yard and come see me?" Maggie grimaced at the offer of the check coverage. There was no way she was going to write a bad check.

"I will call you as soon as I can get to town. Will you be in all week?"

"For the most part, so just call first. I'm sure we can work something out. Is that brother of yours coming too?"

"No, Robert is still in Chicago."

"That's too bad. He has a fine head on his shoulders."

"Um, yea. Mr. Jensen, I'll call you for an appointment as soon as I can."

"That's fine, Maggie. It will be good to see you again." Maggie hung up the phone and scowled.

So that's the way it is. I'm a girl and incapable of handling finances. Is your brother coming? Oh. Too bad. Grrr.

As the afternoon wore on, the humidity abated somewhat as everything began to dry out. She had just decided she was tired of fighting mosquitoes and flies when someone turned into the lane and got out of the truck. When she realized it was her neighbor Joe, she walked through the yard to meet him halfway. "My lord, Maggie. What a mess. I see you still have the house."

"Come see. I lost the back porch, but there's a lot of damage." As they walked toward the house, Joe surveyed the damage. They stopped by Maggie's desk set up, and Joe stared at the house.

"This can't be good. Is it safe for you to be in there?"

"Actually, everything seems to be intact except this outside wall. There hasn't been any shifting, and I've been in and out of there several times. I slept in my own bed last night, but I have no electricity or anything right now. I doubt the electric company will hook me up until someone takes care of the hole in the wall. The trees are in front of the shop where the car and truck are, and as you saw for yourself, I can't get down the lane. It's too muddy to cut across the yard or go around in the fields."

"Listen, why not pack a bag and come home with me? We have a guest room with its own bath you can use until you have electricity again. Sheila will love it, and the kids can get to know a new auntie. What do you say?"

"Are you sure Sheila will be okay with it? After all, that's not leaving her much time to say no."

"It's fine. I'll give her a call while you pack your bags. You want this laptop and file to go?" Maggie looked at her set up.

"Yes, I do. I need to take that to the banker when I get ready to meet him. If you'll take that to the truck, I'll take this stuff in and get a bag." Joe grabbed her items and headed for the truck to call Sheila. Maggie grabbed her little table and chairs and then the TV stand and tucked everything back into the house. She went downstairs and packed an overnight bag and grabbed her toiletries. She thought it would be great to get a shower before bed tonight. Her stomach rumbled with hunger. *And get fed too.* Maggie chuckled as she grabbed up her things and closed the bedroom door. She went back upstairs and unplugged the AC and shut the rooms off in case of animals or birds deciding to visit while she was gone. She looked around to make sure the light switches were also off. If her electricity came on and she wasn't here, the last thing she needed was a short in the wiring.

Maggie threw her bag in the back and jumped into Joe's truck. He offered to drive her by all of her holdings so she could look at each section. Maggie noticed that only the land closest to the house had been wiped out by hail or the tornado. There was hope for some income from a couple of the other renters, but it wouldn't be in time to pay the taxes. As they arrived at Joe and Sheila's, Maggie felt relieved to have a complete roof over her head for the night. Once she was settled in her room and had taken a long hot shower, she was ready to help Sheila with supper and help keep an eye on the kids. They were rambunctious and enjoyed having someone else in the house to attract attention to their antics. Once the kids were settled into bed that evening, Joe, Sheila, and Maggie sat in the living room with a cold glass of tea and talked about the storm. Maggie explained how Seth Johanssen was going to bring a crew by to take down the barn, but now that both that and the chicken coop were gone, she hoped he would work on the house. She explained how she met Luke Johanssen and that she was considering hiring him to help her do some other repairs. "So do you know the Johanssens?" Joe grinned.

"They are good people. The kind you like to have on your side. And they do great work. You won't be disappointed in any of them that work for you. I've gotten to know Luke the last couple of years, and he is very dependable. You won't be sorry if you hire him to help. And Seth will probably bring a whole crew over to take care of those trees and tarp the house. He knows what needs done without asking."

Maggie felt instant relief. "Do you guys know William Jensen the banker?" Joe and Sheila looked at each other, then at Maggie.

"Is that the banker you are going to go see?" Maggie saw the reservations her friends had at hearing the banker's name.

"Well, that's whom Dad used, so I thought it was the simplest. I had a strange conversation with him on the phone today and came away believing he didn't want to talk to a female about money. Are there other problems?" Joe glanced quickly to Sheila.

"We just didn't get along with him very well and changed banks. He really isn't agriculture minded and seems to have his own interests in play. But that doesn't mean he won't help you out. After all, your dad used that bank, so maybe he will treat you fine."

"Well, I guess I can always change banks, but I don't have a lot of time before the bills are due." Maggie explained about the financial problems that her father caused but left out the tax issue. Good neighbors and friends were one thing, but to burden then with her father's lapse in judgment was a whole other issue. Besides, she knew that as farmers they had their own financial problems over the years.

"Anyway, Robert and I are working on it, and I still have some money in the bank to start paying all those debts. Even if I can't pay them off, I can pay a good portion and hopefully take care of the rest when the crops come in." They sat and talked about the kids, how Maggie would be looking for a new teaching position locally if she stayed, and a variety of other things before everyone finally decided to call it a night.

Joe yawned. "Sorry, ladies. I have to get up early and get back to work." They all said good night, and Maggie made her way to the spare room, which was on the opposite side of the house as everyone else's rooms. It was peaceful and decorated in a soothing shade of pale blue. It had matching gingham curtains and bedspread. She smiled as she settled in for the night, grateful to have been reunited with great friends.

In the morning after a hectic breakfast and Sheila shooing the kids out into the yard, Maggie called Luke Johanssen and asked if he had been able to reach his father about the house. He said he had and that his father would be over today with a crew to work on the trees and another crew to tarp up the house. Maggie mentioned where she was staying, and Luke agreed to call her when she was able to return home to get her car or truck. "And, Luke, I really would like to keep you on part time, but it's going to be a bit before I know what I'm going to need. I have to wait for the adjuster on the house before I do anything major with it."

"That's fine, Maggie. I'm always around. Just keep my father in mind when you are ready to rebuild the house. He will do a fine job for you at a reasonable price."

"I appreciate that. I'll wait to hear from you before I catch a ride over to get my car." Maggie hung up and called the bank. She requested to make an appointment anytime on Thursday. The receptionist stated she would get back to her later that day with a time.

Maggie went to the guest bedroom and sat at a small desk in the corner and worked on how to divide up the bills. She wrote out two checks to pay off the companies that weren't willing to wait and then spent the next hour trying to find a way to divide the balance of her funds fairly with the other creditors. There were too many bills and just not enough money in the bank. She put away the checkbook and prepared the two checks for mailing. Maggie hoped that the trip to the bank was going to go better than her gut told her it would. An hour later, the bank called and stated that Mr. Jensen wouldn't be available until the following week. Maggie sighed and took the Wednesday appointment down. She thanked the receptionist for her time and hung up. Something just wasn't sitting well with her about this whole banking business. She decided to call Robert later that night and keep him abreast of things. Maggie had sent him a few pictures of the place while she was sitting in the yard whiling away the day, and she had yet to hear back from him.

It was eight that evening before Luke called Maggie to let her know that the trees were finally cleared from in front of the shed and she would be able to drive down the lane to get in and out of the yard. The other crew had gotten several tarps nailed to the house to seal it off, but not before they had to chase a couple of birds out that thought the kitchen would be a good place to start a nest. Maggie thanked Luke profusely and asked to pass her appreciation off to his father. She looked forward to working with them all at a later date. When she told Joe and Sheila that she could go get her car, Sheila offered to take her over the following day. "That way I get to see what happened to the house and trees. I'll miss that barn. We had so much fun jumping from the haymow into the straw pile." They all laughed and talked about many of the other things they used to do as kids until they were all yawning and ready for bed.

Maggie stood up. "I don't know why I'm so tired. I really didn't do anything today."

"The country air will do that to you. Besides, you've had a lot of stress in your life this last month." Joe reached over and patted her on the shoulder on the way to his room. Sheila stood up and hugged Maggie. "Just remember we are always here for you. Now head to bed."

"Yes, Mom!" Sheila swatted at her as they separated and went to their own rooms for the night. Maggie was tired enough that she decided not to call Robert. She felt that if he had any time to do research and had found out anything, then he would give her a ring. Maggie prepared for bed and was once again grateful for a clean bed and great friends.

The next morning while waiting for Sheila to round up the kids and get them ready for a ride to her house, Maggie went online and checked the regulations for the back taxes. What she found didn't bode well for her. She was going to have to get the money fast, because once the three-year mark hit, she only had six months to pay the back taxes plus a 14 percent interest penalty. By all rights, their father should have left her and Robert a healthy inheritance, but having to pay a quarter of a million dollars in back taxes was enough to scare anyone off. It was almost July, and she only had until the end of August. She could sell off a half section of ground and take care of everything, but Maggie not only hated to break up the farm; the area farmers were fighting with low corn prices for the last two years and didn't have the money flowing as easily as the last several years. Having discussed local farming with Joe the last few days, he stated he was cutting back expenses just as many of the neighbors were. He had casually mentioned that he didn't know anyone that was buying land this year, and Joe wasn't sure how much he planned on leasing the following year. It would all depend on the fall harvest and grain prices.

Maggie grabbed her overnight bag and toiletries and headed out to the kitchen where she could hear the morning rush happening. "Need any help in here?" Maggie looked around at everyone in a different state of dress. She began to chuckle, then started to laugh, and eventually she was rolling with laughter at the scene in front of her. Everyone looked at her, and the longer Maggie laughed, everyone else began laughing too. It felt good to laugh and playfully tickle the kids as they worked to get dressed. By the time everyone had calmed down, Maggie had finished getting everyone ready for the quick drive to her place while Sheila finished getting herself ready to go.

Maggie showed everyone around the farmyard, and they all stood back and looked at the house neatly buttoned up with huge blue tarps. As they continued to walk around, Maggie walked to the shop and opened the doors to both the car and the truck. As she walked by the car, she noticed the locked trunk once again. "See that trunk? I found it under some stuff the other day, and when I went to open it, it was locked. I was filthy from all the dirt getting to it, and I still don't know what's in it." Maggie checked behind her to make sure the kids were still safe as they were running around the farm-yard. Sheila looked at the trunk and shrugged her shoulders.

"Looks like a typical old trunk to me. What do you think is in it?"

"I have no idea, but either I run across a key one of these days, or I'm going to bust the lock!" Maggie shook the lock and then wandered out of the shed. She chased the kids around the yard for a while before Sheila gathered her flock and loaded them back in the car for home.

"Come over for the Fourth if you don't have any other plans. We always buy a few fireworks and have a great BBQ. We call and invite friends and neighbors to join us. What do you say?"

"Sounds great. Let me know what time to come over and what to bring. I can help you prepare stuff or keep an eye on the kids while you do it. Either way I have no plans this year."

"Awesome! See you in a few days. Stay safe!"

Maggie looked around. She made her way to the front door. It felt weird using it as they had always used the back door. The front door was "for company" to use. Just as she opened the door, she heard loud trucks out on the road. The electric company was steadily making its way down her road. A pickup turned in and pulled up in front of the house. Maggie went back down the steps to meet the linesman. "I see you have a problem with the house. Do you care if I inspect it to see if we dare hook you back up to the power? We have all the lines back up except for this last mile."

"Come on in. I haven't gone in to check on things since the crew tarped the house. The tornado took the porch off and opened up the front of the house, but everything else has been stable." Maggie showed him in and gave the lineman a tour of the damage. After he reviewed and concurred that the structure damage was limited to the front and checked her electrical boxes, he agreed to hook her up.

"We should be done later this evening, and you will know when you're hooked up because I'm sure every light in the house was probably on before losing power."

"Well, I doubt that, but I'll be able to hear the refrigerator kick on for sure. Speaking of which, I've got to dump the remains of that mess!" The lineman left her to her dirty work, and the electric company began stringing line and placing new power poles.

Maggie turned to the refrigerator and grabbed the trash can. She held her breath as she opened the door and pulled everything out and dumped it in the can as fast as she could. Maggie closed the bag and yanked it out of the trash can and ran for the door. She gasped for clean air as she hit the door and waited to catch her breath. The trash bag was heavy with jars and tubs of old food. Maggie hauled it to the barrel and tossed it in. When she returned to the house, she propped the refrigerator door open to let it air out, then checked the freezer. There was only a half-eaten carton of ice cream, and it had run all over. *I'll clean that up another day.*

Maggie grabbed her bag from outside on the sidewalk and took it down to her bedroom. She left the door open for some air circulation now that she knew there wouldn't be any critters coming in. Since it wasn't quite as hot today, she thought she might as well sit outside and watch the crew work on the lines. She grabbed her phone and a chair and went to sit under her favorite tree. The next thing she knew someone was tapping her on her shoulder and softly calling her name.

Maggie let out a little screech and jumped out of her chair. "My gosh! You scared me!" Looking back with a smile on his face was Luke Johanssen.

"I'm sorry. I was trying to be gentle, but I can't believe you didn't hear me drive in. My bad muffler doesn't allow me to drive in stealth mode." Maggie rubbed her sleepy face and got her bearings.

"I didn't realize I had fallen asleep. I was watching the lineman work, and I guess the heat of the day lulled me to sleep. I didn't sleep the best last night worrying about things. What are you doing here?"

"I was in the neighborhood and thought I would see if you made it home in one piece. Is there anything I can do for you before I go? I've got a few minutes."

"Actually, there is one thing you can do. Come to supper with me. I have no food, and I hate to eat alone."

"I'm in my work clothes, but if you don't mind Ole's place, I'm good with that."

"That would be great. Let me grab my purse. How about I meet you there, and then we can go our prospective ways after supper?"

"Sounds good. I'll see you in town, and I'll get a booth for us."

"Great! I'll break out the truck and be right behind you." As Luke left and Maggie listened to the sounds of the muffler rumbling, she was amazed she hadn't heard him drive in. *Man. I must have really been out.* She shook her head and went to the house to get ready for a quick night on the town. As she ran out the door, she laughed when she thought of locking up what with the tarps all over the place. She jumped into the truck to leave and looked over at the locked trunk. *I've got to figure out where that key is.*

Maggie was only a few minutes behind Luke when she found a place to park and flew into Ole's Big Game Steakhouse. The place was iconic, and people traveled far and wide to see the place. In the old days, Ole had travelled the world and brought back many types of animals, had them stuffed, and they were all put on display. You were greeted by a huge polar bear as you entered, and it was nothing to watch people spend an hour wandering the café, looking at all of the types of animals on display. Ole had been gone for several years, but the new owners kept the magic going. Maggie found Luke waving her over to their booth, and she settled in for a quiet supper. As they each sat holding a menu and discussing options for supper, across the room talking about her were two men in their own booth. If Maggie had noticed them, the red flags would have been flying. Quietly moving away from her line of sight and out the door, Gary Johnson and William Jensen managed to escape unnoticed.

CHAPTER 4

The Fourth of July was on a Saturday this year, and Maggie had spent the few days before cleaning up the house and packing up her father's clothes. She had more than enough time to burn since the adjuster wouldn't arrive until after the holiday, and the banker wouldn't see her until the following Wednesday. As she lovingly went through the closet and dresser, packing up items she remembered seeing her father wear, nostalgia hit her. She would see her father in certain outfits and smile as she remembered past events and celebrations for each dress shirt or jacket. He didn't have a large variety of clothes, and most of them were threadbare. Maggie made two piles—one to take to the trash, and the other to give to the thrift shop or Goodwill.

When she finished with the clothes, she opened a side chest that sat in the corner of the room for as long as she could remember. As she opened one drawer and then another, she was confused at the contents. When she realized what she was looking at, Maggie was very surprised over her findings. Every drawer contained something of her mother's. The top drawer held her jewelry, including her wedding band. The second drawer was filled with a few scarves and mementos. The third drawer was full of mail. As Maggie sifted through the envelopes, she realized that the letters were from her parents to each other as they were courting. One pile was tied in a pink ribbon and the other tied with a blue ribbon. Maggie smiled and left them in the drawers. It felt like it might be sacrilege to disturb or read them right now as the wound was still too fresh from her father's death. There was one more drawer, but Maggie didn't open it right away. Finding her mother's things caused too much emotion to bear on top of everything else. Maggie boxed up the good clothes and took it out to the living room coffee table. She went back and made several trips to the trash with the other clothes and items that were no longer of use. She kept a few old T-shirts for cleaning rags. Maggie was happy for the distraction of the Fourth of July before dealing with any more memories in the house.

The weather report for the Fourth was hot and sunny, and Maggie was tickled to be able to spend it with friends. She offered to arrive early and help make the potato salad and keep the kids occupied as Sheila and Joe set up for the party. They had invited a few good friends over, and Sheila told her that she would probably know most of them. Since she was going to stay in the neighborhood, Maggie thought it was a wonderful opportunity to get reacquainted with old friends and make some new ones. She had been holed up at the farm far too long.

As early evening arrived, so did the guests. Maggie was introduced to several couples and immediately became reacquainted with old friends. As they were rounding up all the kids to provide their meals first, a late arrival was heard driving in. Maggie said she would go invite them to the back yard as Sheila was busy trying to keep her kids corralled long enough to fill their plates. As she walked out of the back gate, Maggie realized it was Luke. "What a nice surprise! Come on to the backyard. I didn't know you were coming tonight." Luke looked surprised to see Maggie too.

"Yea. Joe invited me over last week. I had an emergency repair call at the last minute, so that's why I'm late."

"You're just in time. They're getting the kids served first, and Joe is flipping hamburgers and grilling hot dogs left and right." Maggie led him to the backyard and offered him a bottle of water before going to help Sheila with her kids. Luke looked around and walked to the grill to find Joe.

As the kids finished their meals and were allowed to once again run free, the teens took them to the side yard and helped the smaller kids use sparklers and smoke bombs. The adults sat around, talking and reminiscing. Maggie visited with several old friends and caught up on what was happening in their lives. She told them of her possibility of staying at the farm but still wasn't sure what would happen. Maggie didn't want to discuss financial issues, so she mentioned she had to settle the estate and then see what she wanted to do in the future.

Maggie sat down on a bench with a cold drink. She felt someone sit beside her. As she looked over, she realized it was Luke. "Hey. I haven't talked to you at all tonight. How are you?" He looked over at Maggie with a smile. "I was beginning to think you were ignoring me." Maggie shook her head.

"Nope. Just catching up with old friends and making new ones. It's been a great day." Before Luke could respond, Joe began the fireworks display. For an hour, the men provided the group with a wonderful show and the kids oohed and aahed along with their parents. When it was over, some of the parents with the smaller children gathered up their belongings and said a quick good-bye and stated their thanks for the great evening, wishing they could stay longer but needed to the little ones home to bed. Other friends hung around and visited for a while as the teens offered to clean up the debris.

Maggie got up to leave, and Luke joined her as she said her good-byes and promised to stop by soon. Luke told Maggie he would walk her to her car and thanked Joe and Sheila for the great evening.

Maggie walked slowly to the car, looking up at the stars. Occasionally, in the distance, they could see someone else was shooting off their own fireworks. "Thanks for walking me to my car, Luke, but it wasn't necessary." Maggie leaned back on her car door, looking at the sky. Luke leaned back beside her.

"Maggie, I'd like to take you out for supper this next week." Maggie jerked her head toward Luke.

"You mean, a date?" Luke glanced back and then at the sky again.

"Yea. I really enjoyed our supper at Ole's the other night, and I would like to get to know you better. Can I call you the first of the week and set a time?" He looked back at Maggie, who was still staring at him. She was totally taken by surprise.

"I guess so. That would be nice. I get pretty tired of my own company these days." Luke frowned at her response. Maggie realized how that must have sounded. "I'm sorry, Luke. That didn't come out right. I just meant, well, you know." Maggie was frustrated and angry at herself. A perfectly nice gentleman asked her out, and she acted like she accepted it out of boredom. Maggie looked back at Luke. "I apologize. I would love to go to supper with you and get to know you better too. I am evidently pretty rusty in the dating department." Luke reached out and took Maggie's hands.

"It's okay. I think I understand. I'll call you in a couple of days." With that, Luke walked to his truck and left the driveway. Maggie waited a few minutes and gathered her thoughts, and with one last look at the stars, she got in the car to drive home.

Joe and Sheila were standing by the corner of the house and watched the exchange. Sheila reached over to Joe and gave him a hug. "What do you think?" Joe smiled. "I think it looks pretty good from here." He grabbed Sheila's hand and walked her back to the rest of the guests.

Maggie got up in time for church the following day and decided to sit in the old family pew. After talking to a few parishioners, she found her way down the aisle and sat down. As she settled in and was reading the bulletin, she felt someone sit beside her. As Maggie looked over, she realized it was Gary Johnson. *What the heck?* she thought.

He smiled and greeted her. "How are you this morning?"

"I'm fine. You?"

"Good. Great in fact."

"I thought you sat in the back all the time?"

"I usually do, but thought I would join you today." Maggie felt a chill go up her spine.

What was it that bothered her about him? she thought. As the service was just beginning to start and they stood up to sing, Maggie grabbed her things and left the pew and went to sit by an elderly couple who had been friends of the family for years. Gary looked shocked at her leaving the pew and turned and frowned at her. Maggie enjoyed the service and tried not to look at Gary. Afterward, she stayed in the pew and visited with the couple until the church was almost empty. As the three left and said good-bye to each other and the pastor, Maggie started for the car. As she glanced up to where her car was parked, she saw Gary standing beside it, arms crossed with a grimacing look, eyes dark and cold. Startled and feeling a chill return, she stood tall and stared at him.

"What can I do for you?" Maggie reached into her purse for her keys as she asked. She glanced down to grab the keys, and when she looked up, Gary was still staring at her.

"I don't appreciate you making a fool of me in church. Why did you leave me in the pew like that?"

"Why did you sit by me in the first place?"

"I want to get to know you better, and for some reason, you are ignoring me. What seems to be your problem?"

"I don't know what your problem is, but my problem is I want to get in my car and leave, so move yourself out of the way. Now please." They stood staring at each other for a few seconds. Maggie's stare never wavered, and Gary finally stepped aside. "Thank you." Maggie unlocked the car and got in, locking it immediately as she slammed the door. She left the parking lot quickly and looked in her rearview mirror. Gary was still standing there, glaring at her with his arms still crossed. Maggie looked back to the road and headed for home. She picked up her phone and called her brother, hands shaking.

"Robert. I'm glad you answered. I just had the weirdest conversation with that Gary fellow. He's scary! I actually felt threatened at church."

"What the heck?" Maggie relayed the conversation and how Gary had been blocking her car door. "I haven't had much time to check on him. I'll get right on that this week. Stay away from him if at all possible."

"I'm trying. I may have to change churches or not go. That seems to be the only place I see him anyway."

"Did you ever get a lock on the back door? Oh, wait. You don't have a back door anymore." They both chuckled, but Maggie reassured him that the front door still had a lock on it and she was using it.

Maggie caught Robert up on the appointments coming up with the bank and the adjuster and talked about her concerns. Maggie always had good instincts about people, and Robert trusted that what she was feeling about Gary Johnson and William Jensen was spot-on. He put a note in his date book to have some research completed soon on them both. They also decided Maggie should talk to a real estate agent about selling some land if the meeting at the bank didn't go well.

"Maggie, let me know if I need to come back and kick someone's butt for you."

They both laughed as Robert had never kicked anyone's butt his whole life. They agreed to call each with any additional news they received. Maggie was almost home by the time she hung up and stopped shaking from her encounter with Gary Johnson.

Maggie spent the next few days making sure her information for the banker was complete. Wednesday arrived, and Maggie planned to make it a full day. After seeing the banker, she would get a week's worth of groceries before coming home. The adjuster wouldn't make it until the following day, and Luke had called to set up a Friday night supper date. She was confident by then she would know if she was going to have enough money to work on the house, and her list of repairs for Luke was growing. Since the tornado, most of the structures sustained some damage, and if she was going to keep them for use in the future, Maggie wanted to save them now. She showered and dressed in business attire, followed by a small application of makeup. The sun had given her a warm glow and only required a little gloss and mascara.

As Maggie pulled up to the bank, her nerves began to get the best of her. She looked in the rearview mirror and gave herself a pep talk, opened up the car door, grabbed her files, and attempted to look confident walking into the bank. Maggie introduced herself to the receptionist and was directed to the waiting area by the front wall. As she sat down in the hard chairs, the receptionist picked up the phone and notified Mr. Jensen that she was there.

"He'll be with you momentarily."

Maggie thanked her and sat looking around the bank. It was a small building and had been there as long as she could remember. Mr. Jensen hadn't joined the bank until about the time she graduated from high school. As she thought back, she could remember her dad scowling after a visit to the bank and mumbled something about the new banker being on his high horse. Her father never said anything bad about anyone, so it took her by surprise. Maggie looked down at her watch and realized she had been sitting there almost a half hour. First, she was surprised how quickly time flew while she was day-dreaming but became agitated at not knowing why she had to wait so long. Maggie thought about their previous conversation and began to think it was being done on purpose. She knew he didn't want to deal with her, but being rude wasn't helping her opinion of him.

After forty-five minutes, Mr. Jensen finally came out of his office and walked over to the coffeepot, fixed himself a cup, and stood there drinking it while looking out the window. Maggie looked at the receptionist, and she was visibly nervous and embarrassed by the obvious snub. Maggie gave her a small shrug and smile, which seemed to relieve the receptionist's guilt. Once the cup of coffee was down, Mr. Jensen looked over at the receptionist and told her to send Ms. Chesney in. Maggie chuckled. "I believe I heard him. Don't worry about it." Maggie had never been treated so poorly before but would ride this visit out. She walked confidently into Mr. Jensen's office and extended her hand. "Mr. Jensen, good to see you again. Maggie Chesney." After a quick handshake, Maggie sat down and faced the banker.

"Well, now. You wanted to talk about some funds. Do you have anything I can review to show you actually need a loan?"

Maggie handed a copy of the file she had made. "This lists all the creditors and the amount due. I also included a current copy of the bank statement even though I know you have that available. I have also included a copy of the letter from the courthouse on the back taxes. As you can see, I would need to borrow a significant amount of money."

The banker closed the file. "You are not employed. How in the world do you think you will pay this money back?"

"The land lease income will come due this fall, and I have at least two sections that will produce and another two that will have some income as soon as the insurance adjuster stops by. I'm confident that with the new leases starting next year that the loan will be covered sufficiently. And, of course, the value of the land itself can be held for collateral." Maggie found herself holding her purse so tight her fingers were starting to hurt. She tried to loosen her grip and continue to smile at the banker.

"I see. Well. First things first. Here is the paperwork that you must fill out before the bank considers any loan. You can get that back to me when they are completely filled out. The board doesn't meet until the twenty-ninth of the month. With the amount of money we are discussing, it has to go to the full board for approval." Mr. Jensen shoved the paperwork across the desk to her. Maggie picked it up and quickly looked at it.

"I can have this back to you next week. Is there anything else you need?"

Mr. Jensen looked at her sternly. "I suggest you find a job and give up the farm. I don't think this loan will go through, but it's not up to me. I don't know why you would want to keep it anyway. Your father hasn't deposited much money in this bank for years, so I doubt you can prove your leases would pay off a loan of this size."

Maggie sat back with her mouth gaping open as she realized what he was saying. She shut her mouth, stood up, and nodded at Mr. Jensen. "I see." She reached over and picked up her file. "I'll just take this with me."

"I'll need that back along with your loan papers all filled out."

"I understand, Mr. Jensen. Good day."

Maggie turned on her heels and left the bank. As she got in the car and slammed the door, the anger continued to spill over, and she wanted to scream. As she was sitting out in public, she thought better of it. Maggie pulled out and sat at the stop sign longer than necessary to get her thoughts and emotions under control. The next step was checking with a realtor. Maggie had a friend from high school who was selling real estate and decided to go see her next. As she pulled up to the office, she could see Jessie inside talking to someone. Maggie collected her thoughts and gave herself a few moments since Jessie was busy. She formulated how she wanted to present the idea of selling off some land without sounding desperate. Just as she was getting ready to get out of the car, she noticed Gary Johnson leaving the office and heading down the street. He was swaggering and preening as he walked. Maggie paused before getting out, not knowing what to think of the visit. It did give her pause. She got out of the car and walked into the real estate office. "Jessie?"

"Maggie? Oh my gosh! How are you?" Jessie rushed over to give her old friend a hug. "Come on over here and sit down. What are you doing these days?"

As the old friends caught up on their lives, Maggie looked at her watch. "Look at the time. I need to get going, but I wanted to ask you about selling off some property."

Jessie looked startled for a second. "What property are we talking about?"

"I would like to sell a half section of land on the southwest corner of the farm."

Jessie chewed on her pencil top for a bit. "I see. You realize that land isn't selling well these days. I barely sell houses due to the economy. If my husband didn't have a good job, I'd have to close up shop."

"So you don't think you can find someone, say, in the next thirty days?"

Jessie looked startled. "Oh, heavens no! Until the crops come in this fall, no one will be looking to buy anything. I mean, I could try, but it really doesn't look good right now."

Maggie felt her stomach drop. "I knew things were tight, but I figured you would know someone."

"Well, Gary Johnson is a land broker, and he buys land. Plus, he might know someone that is looking."

"I saw him in here when I pulled up."

"You did? Oh yea. That. He stops by now and then to see if I have a good lead on something for him." Jessie looked a little nervous.

Maggie cocked her head and looked at Jessie. "And do you?"

"Do I what?"

"Have a good lead for him?"

"Oh. No. No. I don't. I mean, I do now with you sitting here. I'll be sure to tell him you want to sell some land. I'm sure he will be interested."

"I see. Thanks anyway, Jessie. It was good to see you again. If you hear of anyone other than Gary Johnson, you can call me. There's no sense in writing up a contract when you're so sure I can't sell right now."

"I'm sorry, Maggie. I'll let you know! But I don't know why you don't want me to tell Gary. He comes in here all the time to ask about land. I should shut my mouth occasionally as sometimes he runs out and buys land from under me, and I don't get my commission. He sure is good-looking, though!"

Maggie turned to leave, then looked over her shoulder. "You were a good friend in school, Jessie. A real good friend. I don't want Gary Johnson to know anything about my property." With that, she walked out the door and drove off. Jessie was left staring after Maggie.

Maggie drove over to the grocery store and bought enough groceries to get her by for the next several days. She wasn't too anxious to return to town anytime soon. When she returned home and had the groceries put away, she changed into her jeans and T-shirt, grabbed an ice tea, and went to sit out under her favorite elm tree. She sat and thought about the day and how it became stranger as the day progressed. She was going to wait until the adjuster had showed up before calling Robert, but the day was so bizarre she wanted to speak with him this evening. As she waited for him to get home from work,

Maggie got up and walked to the pond. The evening was still quite warm, but there was a gentle breeze blowing that lifted her hair off her neck and cooled her. She stood with her iced tea, watching the frogs catching mosquitoes and other flying creatures as the sun began to slowly glide toward the horizon. Maggie walked back toward the house but stopped in the shed where the trunk was still sitting there stubbornly locked. She shook her head and went on up to the house to call her brother.

As Maggie relayed the day's events, Robert became more agitated. He had someone helping him try to find information on both the banker and the land agent, but they were both busy with their workloads, and it was difficult to find the time to complete the searches. When Maggie offered to do some research, Robert told her that he thought it safer for him to do it since he was out of town and no one would know they were looking into their backgrounds. Robert promised that he would have more information by the weekend or at least by the first of the week.

"Keep your chin up, sis. I know we only have seven weeks to figure this out, but I'll do my best to help find a way."

"I appreciate it, Robert. I really do. I don't know whether to fix the place up or let it be since I might have to move out."

"I hadn't thought of that. If the house is buttoned up tight enough, you better not put any more money into it until we know if we can save the farm."

"That's what I was thinking. I guess I'll concentrate on the old bills. Dad has enough to pay part of it, and I can take the rest from savings. That way if I have to walk away, I won't feel guilty about leaving people high and dry."

"Maggie, I'll send you a check for part of that. It's the least I can do for being the wayward son."

"Are you sure?"

"Yes, I'm sure. The place was left to both of us, and I don't want you to touch your savings. You know us Chesneys. We always pay our debts."

"Thanks, Robert. If we find a way to keep the place, I'll pay you back tenfold."

"I doubt that, but it's a nice thought. I'll talk to you as soon as I know something."

After their conversation, Maggie felt a little better about her day. She had no intentions of going back to Mr. Jensen, Jessie, or Gary Johnson. Once she heard back from Robert, they would plan their next move. In the meantime, she would continue to box up her father's personal things and look in every nook and cranny for the missing keys to the trunk in the shed. If she lost the place, she wanted to be prepared to walk away. Maggie had called her landlord after she decided to stay on at the farm and requested a month-to-month lease since she didn't know how long she would be gone. The annual lease had been due, and her landlord was happy to work with her. Maggie had lived in the same apartment for five years and had left everything there when she quit her job. She didn't know what her long-term plans were going to be and still didn't. Maggie did have her mail forwarded, but most of the bills were automatically taken out of her account anyway, including her rent. The only consolation was she at least had a place to go to if she lost the farm.

Maggie spent the next day alternating on packing things away and waiting for the adjuster. Mr. James finally arrived midafternoon and took notes and pictures of the house. After answering a dozen questions about the storm and what it had done to the whole farm, he sat at the kitchen table in front of the AC and drank iced tea while he worked diligently on his forms. When he had completed his paperwork, he sat back and took several gulps of his tea. "I appreciate you offering me a cool place to sit while I work on this. And thanks for the ice tea. Not everyone is as accommodating."

"You're welcome, Mr. James. I'm just glad you were finally able to make it. I know there was a lot of damage around the community."

"Yes, there was. The damage to your house could have been so much worse too. I'm glad you found someone to seal it up so tightly. Most people throw a tarp on and expect it to stay, but with the winds we get around here, they usually don't."

"I had some great help. The tarps have barely moved, and I'm grateful it has kept the critters out."

Mr. James laughed, then finished off the last of his tea. He tore off a copy of the report and handed it to Maggie. "I'll be honest with you. With your deductible, it's going to be hard to find someone to fix this place for the amount we are going to give you. On top of your five-thousand-dollar deductible, the policy isn't written for replacement cost. I can only give you a fraction due to the age of the home. I suggest that you pay for a better policy once you have made your repairs. I realize things like this happen once in a lifetime, but you really don't want to chance it."

Maggie looked at the paltry amount at the bottom of the form. "It is just one more thing, Mr. James. The problems just keep piling up around here. If I remain here, I will take that information under advisement. Right now, I'm not sure I will be here after the summer is over, but I thank you for your time."

Maggie walked Mr. James out to the car and waved as he drove away. *Just one more nail in the coffin, so to speak.* Maggie shook her head and went back in to finish packing up the den. She was hoping to find anything that might lead her to the answer to the financial mess she was in, but so far, the files were old and useless. Maggie was looking for something that might lead her to a different bank, checking, or savings account. It didn't make any sense. The banker believed her father never took in any money from the leases, but the leases were renewed every year. *So where is the money?*

She packed the paperwork up in the boxes she had brought home from the grocery store. Maggie didn't want to burn anything until she was sure there was no need for them any longer. The drawers of the desk and filing cabinet were empty now, and six more boxes were piled up in the living room, which had become the new storage unit. Maggie sat on the couch looking at all the boxes. She glanced down and saw the old photo album, reached over, and began to thumb through it. Her father had done a nice job putting all of the school pictures in it. Maggie chuckled as she looked at her crooked bangs in one picture and a cowlick in another. Robert's weren't much better with a collar standing up on one side and a scowl in another. Maggie put the album back on the shelf. She'd find a special box for that when the time came.

She went back to the bedroom one more time and opened all the drawers and closets. The bedding was stripped off the bed and the pillows thrown out. There was nothing left except the small chest. She grabbed the sides and moved it to the living room and walked back to shut the door. "Bye, Dad." Maggie slowly closed off the bedroom.

CHAPTER 5

Maggie worked most of the day cleaning the upstairs bathroom and the den. Once everything was thrown out and the linen was washed, she closed the linen closet with a sigh. *One more job down.* The fixtures were old but in pretty good shape. Now that it was all cleaned up, Maggie would feel more comfortable having guests use this bathroom. She had opened a side window to catch a breeze while she worked. The fan blowing cool air from the kitchen didn't help much, but it kept the hallway and living room at a decent temperature. Maggie hung a fresh hand towel next to the sink and shut the light off. She looked at the time and realized she needed to clean herself up next. After all, tonight was her date with Luke.

Maggie hadn't thought about her date over the course of the day as she had been too busy cleaning, and her thoughts ran more toward solving the financial crisis in front of her. Now that she was a couple of hours away from seeing Luke, he was all she could think about. Maggie quickly went to the mailbox to collect several days' mail and then sat at the kitchen table to cool off while catching up on the bills and other notices. Nothing looked very interesting, and most of it was junk. She got up and grabbed a cool glass of water from the tap and downed it. Maggie refilled the glass and went to the basement to get ready. Luke had called yesterday and told her it would be a casual meal but wouldn't say where he was taking her.

Once showered and changed into a pair of khakis and lilac-colored blouse, she looked in the full-length mirror and immediately changed from the khakis to a fairly new pair of jeans. Leaving her hair flowing down her back, she stepped in some dressy slip-ons and was ready for her date with Luke. She was ready early, so she grabbed her purse and the glass of water and went outside to wait for him. The evening wasn't as hot as it had been the last two weeks. A cool front had come through that morning and made the temperatures almost manageable. She was sitting under her favorite elm when Luke arrived.

"Looks like that must be a favorite spot of yours. I think that's the third time I've seen you sitting there."

Maggie smiled. "Of all of the trees out here, I find this one has the best canopy. Even that storm didn't ruin my shade."

"Are you ready to go?"

"I sure am. I'll just leave my glass on my chair, and I can get it tomorrow." Maggie grabbed her purse, and Luke opened the truck door for her. She looked around the truck as she waited from him to get in. "It looks pretty clean for a repair guy."

He looked a little sheepish. "Well, it might have something to do with the fact that I may have cleaned it up a bit today." They both chuckled.

"Where are we going?"

"I thought we'd drive into North Platte and go to the steak house. They have live entertainment tonight, which is a plus."

"Sounds good. Local band?"

"I suppose so. I've never heard of them, but if they're terrible, I guess we can leave early."

"Absolutely."

The two chatted about the scenery, traffic, and the weather for the trip. As they pulled into the parking lot, they both became quiet. Luke came around and helped Maggie out of the high pickup. As they walked to the steak house, she began to feel a little nervous since this was the first date she'd had in a long time.

Once they were settled, looked at the menus, and ordered, the two began questioning each other about their lives growing up. Maggie explained how her mother had died and about her brother not wanting to be a farmer but was successful in his own right. Luke mentioned growing up in a large family. He was the fourth of six and was expected to stay and work with his father, as all the boys had, and it was why they didn't get along since Luke went out on his own. What really upset his family was him leaving the Mennonite Church.

Just as Maggie was going to ask him about it, the food arrived. They began eating and exclaimed how good the food was. Maggie pointed a fork at Luke.

"I never asked, but I assumed that was what your father was. I knew we had a few families in the area that were Mennonites, and there was a church in their neighborhood. So why did you leave the church? That's a pretty drastic step."

"Yea." Luke rubbed the back of his neck, then took another bite. "It's a long story, but the gist of it is I was invited to a different church one time by a friend of mine, and I really liked it. Once I graduated from high school and went on to trade school, I looked for another church similar to it. I left the church while I was away, and when I chose to move back to the area and work, my father really had a hard time with all of it. First, I didn't want to work with him, and now I don't go to church there."

"I can see how that has hurt your relationship."

"Well, it's gotten better. He realizes I'm my own man and can make my own mistakes, so he tolerates me working elsewhere. He may never get over me leaving the church."

"Where do you go?"

"I started to attend New Hope in Ogallala when I moved back."

"I thought about going there on Sunday, actually. I grew up in the local Methodist church, but then I went to college, and when I got my first job, I started attending the Berean Church."

"That would be great if you wanted to go. I can wait for you in the foyer if you want, and we can sit together. I can introduce you to the pastor."

"That would be nice. It's hard to go by yourself, isn't it?"

"Yes, but you don't get distracted as easily, either."

"I guess that is the upside. I like the home church and its pastor, but I'm having a bit of trouble with one of the congregation."

"Really? Tell me about it."

Maggie explained the gut instinct she had about Gary Johnson and how he made her feel. "He just seems dishonest. And after the last confrontation by my car, he scared me. That's when I decided to change churches."

"Wow. You shouldn't have to change churches because of someone that goes there. Wait a minute. Is he the land broker?"

"Yes, why?"

"I've heard grumblings about him, but I never paid any attention to the gossip. I try to stay out of those types of conversations."

"Well, there has been nothing specific I can point out, but he just creeps me out."

Maggie and Luke finished up their meals about the time the band started to play, which put any thought of conversation to a stop. They listened for about a half hour before deciding to leave because it was so loud they couldn't visit.

On the way home, Maggie explained that she was having some financial issues and wouldn't be able to hire him for the much-needed repairs until she knew for sure she was staying at the farm. She explained it would be late August before things would be settled and to please notify his father that she couldn't hire him until fall if she was going to fix the house. Luke understood but offered his services anyway if she needed an emergency repair.

As Luke pulled into the driveway, they agreed to meet for the early service on Sunday morning. "I really enjoyed getting to know you better, Maggie. Thanks for coming out with me tonight."

"I really enjoyed it too, Luke. It was a great night."

Luke walked her up the steps and took her hand and kissed the back of it. "I'll see you Sunday morning." Luke scooted off to the truck and was gone before Maggie could reply. The back of her hand tingled from his kiss. Maggie smiled as she let herself into the house and locked the door behind her. "What a nice man."

Saturday dawned bright and early, and Maggie decided to clean out an old pantry. She was throwing a lot of old cans of food in the garbage when she knocked something over. She looked down and realized it was the .410 shotgun. Her father used it occasionally to shoot at the skunks that tried or would be successful getting into the chicken house. Maggie looked around and found a partial box of shells. She picked up the gun and shells and took them to the table for safety, then continued with her cleaning. As she took the last bag of trash out, she looked back at the gun. Her father had taught her how to use it in case he wasn't home. She took the gun outside and looked down the barrels. It was surprisingly clean. As she checked it over, Maggie realized her father had kept it in fine working order. Maggie went back into the house and retrieved the box of shells. She walked down to the wood pile and set up a couple of targets, loaded the gun, and took the safety off. As she lined up the target, Maggie remembered to pull it tight into her shoulder to absorb the kick. She pulled the trigger, and the noise and kick shocked her. Even though she knew it was going to kick and was prepared for it, her shoulder was already sore. Maggie lined up the second target and fired again. She hit the second target but was ready to quit as she reached up to rub her shoulder. She popped the spent shells out and returned to the house. Maggie put the gun behind the front door along with the shells. She didn't know what she was going to do with it, but with the house exposed as it was, she was glad to have it handy.

After lunch, Maggie decided to go through the paperwork again. She couldn't believe there wasn't a clue where her father had placed his money. Maggie grabbed box after box and looked at every single piece of paper. She found nothing new and the bank statements showed exactly what the banker had said should be in the account. Her father had placed a few thousand dollars in the bank every year, but it was just enough to live on and pay bills for that year. According to the leases, there should have been thousands of dollars available to her, not hundreds. She continued to puzzle on it as she put everything away for the day. If only he had kept the ledgers up, it would have made it so much easier for her.

Maggie overslept Sunday morning and had to rush around to get ready. She still had a thirty-minute drive to make. As she pulled into the parking lot of the church, she saw Luke standing at the front door looking at his watch. She jumped out of the car and hustled to the door. "I'm sorry, Luke. Am I awfully late? I overslept."

Luke smiled. "Right on time." He took her elbow, and they strode to the sanctuary just as the first chords of music were beginning. "I saved us a couple of spots with my Bible."

"Oh, Luke. I forgot mine."

"It's all right. We can share." He led her to their pew, and they settled in as everyone began singing the first praise song.

After church, Luke led Maggie to the pastor and introduced her. There were a few people there whom Maggie knew from when she grew up, and they greeted each other and promised to catch up another day when they all had more time. As they visited with several of Luke's friends, she felt very comfortable in his presence. Luke reached over and took her hand and held it as they walked around visiting. Luke was going to attend his Sunday school class, but Maggie deferred. "This was nice, Luke, but I think I will go home for now and think about it. Thanks for inviting me and showing me around."

"My pleasure, Maggie. My pleasure. I'll call you in a couple of days, all right?"

"Great. Looking forward to it." With that, Maggie left the crowd behind and headed for home, a smile on her face and a song in her heart.

Later that day, she decided to call Robert. Just as she was picking up her phone, it rang. Robert beat her to it. After sharing pleasantries, Robert got right to the reason for the call. "Let me tell you something. This is bigger than you can believe. We are calling the state licensure office and discuss our findings with the real estate licensing people, and then we're calling a bank examiner."

"What the heck are you finding?"

"That's just the problem. We aren't finding anything, and if you are legit, you should be able to find something. There is no such person as Gary Johnson. Nothing. Nada. No wonder you were having a bad feeling about him. Jack and I have been searching everything and everyone. And the people that paid the taxes are a company called Sinclair Land Agency, but again, there is nothing out there on them. I think you have a racket going on there, and the poor people of Paxton are being swindled. I wouldn't put it past the banker to be in on it since that Gary fellow would have to be able to have the funds tucked away somewhere."

Maggie grabbed a chair and threw herself into it. "What a mess. So what are you going to do now? Go over that again."

"Come Monday, Jack and I are going to contact our corporate lawyer and let him handle all of this. The Feds will be more impressed if we have a lawyer contact them and we have everything laid out for the lawyer to hand over. We really wanted to do this ourselves, but after we began to uncover all these discrepancies, we decided a lawyer was required, and we'll have him put a rush on it. I don't want you to do anything, because if everything is legitimate, then you won't be embarrassed, and if it's not, you won't be involved. "

"My gosh. What do you want me to do from here?"

"Just play dumb about it. I just wanted you to know so you could stay as far from everyone as possible. I mailed you a check to help pay Dad's bills, so put it in the bank and get the bills paid. If the banker is crooked, you might have trouble in the long run, but he won't know the difference now. And if he asks you about the loan, tell him you will get the papers to him by the end of the month before the meeting."

"Okay. I can do that. I got a small check from the insurance company for the house, so I will deposit it with yours and have all the checks written out to mail at the same time. That way the money will go in and out pretty quickly. He thinks I'm stupid anyway since I'm a female, so I'll just tell him I'm having trouble filling out all that paperwork."

"Great. Jack and I are on a roll on this end. This is going to take some time, but we'll let the lawyer know we have to have answers before the end of August. He could always file an injunction to buy us time if we need it."

"I'm glad you are handling all of that. I've been going through all of Dad's stuff here and haven't a clue where the money went. I'm going to start visiting the families that are leasing from us and make sure they actually paid Dad. No sense looking for money that isn't there."

"Right. You keep that up. I have no idea what Dad was doing. Maybe he gave it away, but whatever he did, we should be able to track it. Keep looking, Maggie. There has to be a clue there somewhere."

"If we lose the place, I'm going to need you to come out here and help me get the personal stuff out of here. I'm not leaving it to a crook."

"I'll be there if I need to be. You know that. Do you have any-one closer that you can call if you run into any trouble?"

"Well, there is Joe and Sheila, of course, but I do know some-one. His name is Luke, and I was going to hire him to do some repairs, but I've put that on hold. I actually went to supper with him on Friday night."

"Wow, sis. That sounds interesting. Anything more I need to know about this man?"

"Well, not really, but he is a gentleman, and we sat together in church today. I decided to go to Ogallala so I wouldn't run into Gary, and Luke happens to go to that church. He's going to call me later this week."

"Sounds promising. Now I know I'll have to come out there so I can meet this guy."

Maggie laughed. "Well, we'll see how this goes. Right now we are just friends getting to know each other."

"Maggie, since things didn't work out with your college boy-friend, I haven't heard you mention anyone since then, so this could be a possibility, right?"

"Hmmm. I guess I hadn't really thought about that. I've been so busy with my job, and the few dates I've had sure didn't interest me enough to have a second one with them. It could be I just have more free time on my hands right now."

"I doubt it. You actually sounded excited when you told me. I hope this develops into something. You deserve to find happiness like I have. And my kids need cousins to grow up with!"

"Oh, Robert! Stop it. You're embarrassing me!"

"For now I will. Anyway, you take care and stay safe out there."

"I found the .410 yesterday, and I can still shoot. It's by the front door if I need it."

"Well, that sounds pretty drastic, but I guess you never know, and if these guys are seriously hiding something, anything could hap-pen. I'll keep in touch if I find out anything."

"Thanks, Robert. And tell Jack thanks too. I know you two will get this handled."

After Maggie hung up, she sat and stared at the walls. As she thought things through, it began to make more sense. Gary, or whoever he was, was trying to get information from her. He must be the one who paid the taxes since he said he buys and sells land. He would make a fortune by paying the taxes and then selling the land separately. She decided she would stay out of Paxton and only shop in North Platte or Ogallala until Robert had everything figured out. The trip to the bank would probably be on Tuesday, but that would be the last trip she would make to the bank until she had to drop off loan papers. She began to feel a glimmer of hope that things might come together, but she didn't want to get too confident. She needed to make sure the banker thought she was still desperate.

Monday brought a day of rain showers, and it kept Maggie inside. She sat down to the ledger and filled in everything appropriately like her father would have. Then she filled out all the checks and prepared them for mailing. Between the insurance money and Robert's check, she had enough to take care of all the past bills. She didn't want anything hanging over her head in the next six weeks. And one of these days, she needed to visit with the lawyer about settling the estate. Maggie just felt that until the bills were caught up and they knew what to do about the taxes, she couldn't settle anything.

Six weeks. Time was flying. It was early June when their father passed away and only a three weeks since the will was read. Maggie finished the bills and put the envelopes by her purse and wandered through the house. As she entered the den, she looked through everything one more time. Then she pulled the desk and filing cabinet away from the wall. She sneezed from the dust, but there wasn't even a piece of scratch paper to be found. Maggie grabbed the vacuum that was never too far from her cleaning escapades and finished cleaning the den. She shoved the furniture back and looked at the old worn desk. *Where did you put the money, Dad?* Maggie shook her head and proceeded to pull every drawer out and look inside. Not a thing could be found anywhere. She put everything back and took one more look around the empty room and shut another door on her past life.

Maggie felt she had cleaned enough to last a lifetime and decided to grab a book. The rain wasn't going to let up, so she went downstairs and riffled through the selections on the bookshelves. She picked out three and sat on the couch with her pillow and blanket. As she settled into a mystery, she relaxed and found herself deep inside the story line. The next thing she knew the sun was shining through the window and the book was on the floor. When she looked at the clock, it was coming onto ten. She shot up off the couch, and her stomach rumbled. Maggie realized she had read half the night and didn't stop to get supper and was starved. She zipped upstairs and fixed herself a bagel and cup of coffee. As she looked out into the muddy yard, she realized it must have rained hard and long through the night. The mail wouldn't show up until after lunch, so she had plenty of time to get herself ready for the trip to town if Robert's check showed up. Maggie decided she would finish her book this morning and wait until she checked the mail before deciding to tackle the muddy roads.

After finishing her book and fixing a light lunch, she watched the road while she ate to await the mailman. She watched as he slowly drove up to the box and dropped her mail in before leaving. The road looked to be pretty sloppy the way he was driving. The sun was just starting to peek out of the clouds, so it would be another day before the roads would dry out.

Maggie put on her old overshoes to traipse out to get the mail. She leafed through the junk mail and then found Robert's check. As she looked up and down the road, she watched a pickup coming down the road, and he didn't seem to be having any problems. She decided to get the pickup out and take the checks and mail to town.

She prepared the bank slip first and then put everything in her purse. She checked her groceries and decided to pick up a few things too.

Maggie went to the shed and backed the Chevy pickup out carefully. She drove it up to the front of the house, took her overshoes off, and tossed them to the sidewalk, then headed for town. Once she got to the bank, she made a big production of going in and talking loudly to the receptionist and teller as she conducted her business, talking about the rain and how muddy her yard was. Maggie could see that Mr. Jensen was in his office and was listening. Just before she told everyone a cheerful good-bye, Mr. Jensen came out of the office and hollered at her.

"Maggie! Wait up!" Maggie stopped in her tracks and turned around slowly.

"Hello, Mr. Jensen. What can I do for you?"

"I was just checking to see if you brought me some paperwork today. Time is ticking."

"Yes, well, that. I haven't completed it yet. I wasn't in too big of a hurry to get it to you since you aren't having your meeting for a couple of weeks yet, and there are a couple of sections I'll have Robert help me with. I was just conducting some business so I could pay some bills. Thanks for asking. I'll see you soon." Maggie started to leave again.

"Maggie, I don't have time to dally around. You need to get those papers to me soon so I can work on the presentation to the board."

"I see. Well, I don't have all the information you need, so it will take me some time to gather that up. After all, you were the one that told me I couldn't make enough money to pay back that amount of money, so I need to figure that part out. And, of course, Robert has a say in the financial side of the farm too."

"Oh, well . . . you're right, of course. I did say that. Well, then. Get those papers in to me posthaste, will you?"

"Certainly, Mr. Jensen. Good day." Maggie left, and as she got into the truck, she said to herself, "Posthaste? Are you serious?" Maggie shook her head and turned toward the post office. After dropping the payments in the outside drop box, she headed to North Platte for a day of shopping. She was feeling chipper after her little visit and decided she needed a day away from the cleaning and worries of the farm. "Mall, here I come!"

CHAPTER 6

Maggie's shopping spree went well as there were several sales at the mall. The nice thing about shopping in mid-July, everything was going on sale to get rid of the summer stock as they were already bringing in clothing for fall. As she tried on outfits, she would look in the mirror and wondered if Luke would like them. Maggie went home with a variety of outfits suited for working on the farm, going to church, and maybe a date or two with Luke.

The week was going to be spent talking to the families that were leasing the ground. Maggie was continually trying to figure out where her dad's money had gone, and she hoped someone could help her locate it. On Monday, she called each of the four renters and made appointments on separate days through the week and left Joe and Sheila for the last ones to visit with. Sheila invited her over for a Friday night supper, and Maggie was happy to visit with her friends again.

Tuesday evening, Maggie arrived at the Hilman farm and was greeted by two large barking Labradors. She waited until Mr. Hilman came out of the house before opening the car door. The dogs turned out to be quite friendly, and all they really wanted was to be petted and loved by everyone. Their size was the only thing intimidating. Mr. Hilman invited Maggie in and was introduced to his wife,

Vickie. They sat at the kitchen table and made some small talk for a while, getting to know each other a bit, before Maggie changed the subject to the real reason she had made the appointment.

"Mr. Hilman, I have a couple of things I need to discuss with you. First of all, you are leasing two full sections, but you are only using half of them. I was curious as to why you don't have it all planted or why you aren't leasing just one section. Was that a stipulation from my dad?"

"I'm happy to explain. I'm trying my hand at organic farming. In order to do that, I need to go back to the old ways of farming. I leave one field sit for a season and plant another, then do the opposite the next year. It is more time intensive due to weed control, but with the lease your father gives me, it allows me to spend more hours on these fields than in my own. I can get all my other fields planted, then spend the rest of my summer working on your land. It's more expensive, but I get a higher payment in the end. We have a good contract, and as soon as I harvest, it is hauled to a special elevator for storage."

"Organic. Wow. I knew people were looking at that, but I didn't realize it was happening in my own backyard."

"I've been working on it since I started leasing the ground. Your dad hadn't farmed it for a couple of years, so it had gone back to weeds and grass. It took me almost three years before I got it cleaned up enough to produce a good crop, but I've enjoyed every bit of it."

"That's great. I'm glad it is working for you. Are you thinking of expanding it to your own ground?"

Mr. Hilman looked at his wife. "If she had her way, it would all be that way, but it takes a lot of time, and right now, with the kids growing up and needing more things, I can only change to organic a little at a time. I hope you will allow me to continue leasing the ground from you."

"Well, that's one of the things I need to discuss with you. I'm working on a new lease for next year, but I would like to know if you would be interested in buying some of the land you are currently leasing."

The couple looked at each other. "I don't know if you've heard, but the prices we are getting the last couple of years have really dropped, and most of us have stopped buying. We need to save what little we have in case we have emergencies or the prices drop more. Right now, we are operating around breakeven. I told that Johnson guy I couldn't buy that land right now, no matter if it was a bargain price or not."

"Wait. What? Gary Johnson talked to you about buying my land?"

Mr. Hilman looked puzzled. "You mean you didn't contract with him to sell it?"

"I have nothing to do with that man. You mean to tell me he has been going around trying to sell the land already?"

"Well, he came out here a few weeks ago and said it would all be available in the fall and he was lining up buyers. We didn't think much about it since your dad died, and we knew you kids weren't around. Your dad had talked about you being a teacher back east somewhere and that your brother had a career in Chicago. So a land broker offering to sell the land didn't surprise me at all. Not that I liked the guy. He seemed a little oily to me."

"I agree with you there. Well, let me explain what has happened. I feel comfortable talking about it with you as my dad had often mentioned what great neighbors you were." Maggie leaned back and got her thoughts together. "Dad hadn't paid his land taxes for three years, and someone bought them up. If I can't get the funds together by the end of August, I assume that Mr. Gary Johnson will own the farm."

"Are you kidding me? Wait. First of all, I can't believe your dad didn't pay the taxes, but why don't you have enough money to pay them?"

"Exactly the question Robert and I have been asking ourselves since all this came up. Robert is doing some research on Johnson and a couple of others, but in the meantime, I'm trying to find out what Dad did with his money. He left behind several bills, which we've taken care of, but there was only a dab of money in the bank, and all of the statements show him depositing just enough money to get him through the year. So I have to ask you, although this is all so embarrassing, how much have you paid Dad in the last few years, and do you know what he has done with his money?"

Mr. Hilman nodded to his wife, and she got up and left the room. "Hang on, Maggie, and we'll help you with that." Vicki returned with her laptop and loaded up her accounting program. She turned it toward Maggie, and the screen showed her father's name and payments made to him. She outlined the payments and dates for Maggie. Vicki sent the page to her printer so she could have a copy.

Maggie sat back and looked at the Hilmans. "I don't understand. Did Dad ever talk about giving the money away or anything? I haven't found any information from other banking sources."

"I'm sorry, Maggie. He never talked about things like that to me. We only discussed farming and families. Listen. We got our wheat in just before the storm went through, so it was all saved. Vicki can pay you what we owe for the year, and when the corn comes in, we can use that to take care of our other expenses. Hopefully, it will be a good start on getting your funds together to save the place."

As Vicki worked using her computer to write a check and print it off, Maggie sat there feeling quite humbled. "I want to thank you so much for doing this. I'm going to try to come up with enough, but if I can't, I want you to know that I appreciate you having been a good friend to our family."

The Hilmans and Maggie stood up and hugged each other. Mr. Hilman walked Maggie to her car and made sure the dogs were out of the way so she could get in. "Thanks again, Mr. Hilman." Maggie held up the check. "I appreciate this more than you know. Please don't mention any of this to anyone, especially about Gary Johnson. Robert is trying to figure that out, and we don't want him to know we are checking into his background."

"Just keep the place intact. We won't say anything. I know your dad would hate to see someone like Johnson end up with it."

Maggie smiled and waved as she left. She now had a fourth of the money she needed to pay the taxes. She wondered if she would have as much success with the rest of the renters. Getting the check tonight was a surprise, but it set in motion a new wave of hope for her future.

Wednesday, she drove over to the Beal's right after the lunch hour. Mrs. Beal was out of town for a couple of weeks to their daughters because of the arrival of their new grandchild, so Mr. Beal felt that it would be more appropriate for her to show up during the daylight hours. Maggie appreciated him caring about her reputation and on the way over chuckled when she thought about it. Mr. Beal would be around the same age as her father, so she didn't know how much longer he planned on farming. Maggie decided she needed to be as honest with all of the renters as she was with Mr. Hilman. The two sat down and discussed Maggie's dilemma. Again, Mr. Beal stated he couldn't afford any more land, but he was also thinking of retiring soon and didn't know if he would be signing a lease the following year, either.

"I understand, Mr. Beal. I have another question for you. Have you been contacted by Mr. Gary Johnson about buying my property?"

"Yes. A few weeks ago. It was right after your dad died, but by you questioning me about it, I assume you didn't hire him."

"Nope. Well, this is the deal with that." Maggie explained the tax dilemma and how Mr. Johnson fit into the story.

"I'm sorry about the mess you're in. I can't help right now. As you know, I was hailed out in the storm, and I didn't get crop insurance this year on your land. Failure on my part, but it's a crapshoot whether you get a crop or not, and I lost the bet this time."

"I understand. I will either come up with the money, or I won't. Don't worry about it. I appreciate your time." She again asked that he not mention anything about Gary Johnson and the tax issues. He agreed it was nobody's business but hers. The excitement that Maggie felt the day before began crashing down around her as she drove toward home.

Thursday was much of the same with the Camanos. All of their crops were in corn, and they weren't able to pay on the lease until the fall when it was too late. The storm had damaged some of their crops, but they felt that as long as there weren't any further storms, it would produce well. Maggie drove away downhearted. Time was running out. She was down to five weeks. She was anxious to talk to Joe and Sheila the next evening and get their take on everything. Maggie knew that her friends would offer the best advice they could give. Joe's crops were covered by his crop insurance, so she was expecting some money from them, but it would only get her to the halfway point. There was always the attempt to get a loan for the rest. She needed to get the paperwork turned in next week if that was her only option.

Friday late afternoon, Maggie cleaned up and put on some new jeans and a blouse before heading over to Joe and Sheila's place. She had baked a cake earlier in the day and fixed up some homemade fudge frosting. Maggie grabbed the cake pan and headed out, making sure she locked up behind her. After visiting with the neighbors this week, she was becoming more paranoid. Before leaving the driveway, she looked back at the house, the tarps shining in the fading light.

She shook her head as she drove slowly down the lane and headed the car toward what she hoped to be a peaceful evening and questions answered.

Maggie parked the car and picked up her cake pan. Just as she was getting out of the car, the kids ran out of the house to drag her in to their parents. Maggie laughed and allowed the rambunctious children to lead her into their home and had almost dropped the cake pan twice along the way. Sheila shooed the kids to their rooms until supper was ready, and Maggie went with her to the kitchen to catch up and help finish supper. As they finished setting the table, Maggie went to find the kids and call them to supper. She hadn't noticed the extra place setting Sheila had put down, and while she was out of the room, there was a knock on the door. Sheila opened it and invited Luke in.

"Thanks for coming. I'm just about ready to put supper on the table. Joe's washing up. I hope you don't mind, but Maggie is here too, and she's off getting the kids rounded up."

Luke looked pleased at the announcement. "That's great, Sheila. And thanks for inviting me. I've been pretty busy this week, and I'm ready for one of your home-cooked meals."

Luke followed Sheila to the dining room as everyone else converged at the same time. Maggie looked surprised to see Luke.

"Luke! Good to see you! I didn't know you were coming tonight." She looked at Sheila and gave her a look of surprise. Sheila just smiled back and told everyone to have a seat.

The kids all wanted to share sitting around Maggie, and she ended up across the table from Luke, with Joe and Sheila on the ends. Sheila finished bringing the meal to the table, and everyone sat down to a feast. The meal was filled with laughter, and the kids continually had Maggie's attention with stories of spiders, frogs, and TV shows.

After supper, Maggie got up to help Sheila cut the cake and serve it along with some homemade ice cream. Once everyone had their fill, Maggie and Sheila cleaned up the kitchen while Joe took the kids to their room to get them ready for bed. Everyone settled in the living room, and Maggie told the kids bedtime stories. Sheila headed them off to bed, and when she returned, Maggie decided not to put off talking about the farm. It embarrassed her with Luke sitting there listening, but she really didn't want to hide anything from him, either.

"The reason I wanted to meet tonight is to talk about my situation at the farm. I was hoping you could help me talk this out and possibly have some suggestions as to where to go from here." Maggie took a deep breath and began detailing the problems her father left her. She started with getting the letter from the county treasurer, the storms, the visit with the banker, Gary Johnson, and then the visits with her neighbors. As she took a deep breath and looked around, everyone appeared shocked by her revelations. Sheila was nervously wringing her hands, and Joe reached over to put an arm around her shoulders. Luke sat there contemplating the whole scenario.

Joe finally cleared his throat. "Well. No wonder you've been stressed out. First of all, the adjuster was here a couple of days ago, and I have my check ready to deposit. I can go on ahead and pay you just like the Hilmans did, so that should get you halfway to paying the back taxes—just like everyone else, and we talked about this awhile back. We aren't in any position to be buying land. Mr. Johnson hasn't been by our place, but that doesn't mean he won't be one of these days. Rest assured, we have no intention of buying anything from him. Since you have talked to the other renters, I'm sure we can stick together on that, but it won't help if he finds someone somewhere else to buy it. There are some big operators around that are always looking into expanding their holdings."

Maggie sighed. "I appreciate you paying up early. It means a lot to me. I just hope I can figure out a way to get the rest. I'm running out of time."

Luke decided to speak up. "I realize that you don't know me real well yet, but I will talk to my father about this, if it's okay with you, and let him know what Mr. Johnson is up to. The Mennonite community will support you in any way possible and they won't be giving Mr. Johnson the time of day. I'd say you will have a lot of people in the neighborhood preventing an easy sale of your place if you can't find the money."

"I appreciate that, Luke. I hate to let everyone know that Dad wasn't paying his bills, but I'm to the point of no return. Does anyone have any suggestions on how to get the rest of the money?"

Joe leaned over and put his hands on his knees. "I think you'll have to go to the bank. I can't see any other answer. With having half the money in the bank, it should be easier to get the money too. Like I said, if you can't get it from your banker, let me know, and I'll send you to mine."

"I appreciate that, Joe. I don't have a lot of time left. The loan meeting is the twenty-ninth, so I need to get the money in the bank and the adjusted paperwork turned in on Monday. I hope to know the following day whether I got the loan or not. Joe, did Dad ever talk about donating his money or what he might have done with it?"

"No, not a thing. I have no idea what he did with it all. It sounds like he wasn't handling his finances right the last couple of years, but I had no idea he had been slipping."

"I didn't either, and I came to see him frequently. He hid it well. On that note, I better call it a night. I appreciate your candor and let me carry on about my problems."

"No problem. Sheila, would you get the checkbook, and we'll give her a check tonight? Maggie, just don't deposit it until after I get the insurance check in the bank first thing Monday."

Maggie chuckled. "I won't, Joe. I'll go to the bank Monday afternoon, but if something comes up and you don't get to the bank, let me know."

Sheila gave Maggie the check, and everyone walked outside. The night was a little muggy, and the mosquitoes were out. The locusts were buzzing, and occasionally, you could hear a barn owl hoot. They were quiet and listened to the night sounds for a while, lost in their own thoughts. Maggie turned to them all. "Thanks for a great evening. You can get the cake tin back to me later. I won't need it anytime soon, or ever if worse comes to worse."

Sheila gave Maggie a hug, and she got into her car to leave. She waved as she drove out of the yard. Luke turned to look at the couple. "You have any other suggestions?"

"Nope. She needs to figure out if her dad hid the money or spent it. Otherwise, I think the farm is gone. Her banker is a jerk."

Luke was surprised by his comments but took it with a grain of salt. If he had the money, he'd loan it to her in a heartbeat, but that wasn't possible. He really wanted to think of some way to help her. Luke waved good-bye and headed for home. Joe and Sheila walked to the back of the house and sat down in the porch swing to listen to the night sounds. Sheila sighed. "I hope she finds the money, Joe."

Maggie arrived home and realized she had forgotten to turn the porch light on. The automatic yard light was burnt out and was too tall for her to reach with the ladders she had found in the shop. After turning off the car and staring at the house, she thought she saw movement in the trees. She turned the car lights back on and watched but didn't see anything. *I'm really getting paranoid now.* Maggie grabbed her purse, got out, and locked the car as she ran up to the door. She quickly unlocked the door while using the small flashlight on her keychain and then locked it behind her. After catching her breath, she left the lights off and walked to a window that looked out over the yard. As she became used to the darkness, she saw movement far off toward the entrance to the lane but couldn't make out anything. Then it was gone again. Maggie checked all the windows and double-checked the door. She wasn't sure what she saw, but Maggie wasn't taking any chances. After all, the house had a big tarp on it, so it really wasn't all that secure. She grabbed the .410 shotgun and the box of shells and took them with her to the basement where she finally turned a light on. As she prepared for bed, she convinced herself it was probably a coyote and to quit being so anxious. Maggie grabbed a new book to read and settled in until she was tired enough to sleep, the gun close to the bed.

The following day, Maggie returned the gun behind the front door. She decided to leave a couple of shells in it, the safety on. After breakfast, she walked out into the yard and looked around for any type of tracks. She just about gave up when she stumbled across a mark made by a hard-soled shoe. Maggie bent down, studied it, and then attempted to follow the direction she last saw movement. She found a few more and followed the path to the ditch where she lost any traces. As she looked around, she walked over to a row of cedars and looked behind them. There were tracks from a vehicle going from the road to the tree row and then back up to the road. Someone was there last night spying on her. Chills went up her spine. She got her phone out of her pocket and dialed the sheriff's office, explained the situation, and told them to take their time as it wasn't an emergency at that point in time. A deputy would drop out later when he was closer to the neighborhood and take a look at things. Maggie left the tracks behind, and as she walked to the house, she called Robert at work. Things were starting to get ugly.

Robert was in a meeting when she called, but Maggie explained that it was urgent he call his sister back, the secretary stated she would be sure to let him know as soon as he got back to the office. She went back to the house and stood looking at the boxes in the living room. She mentally checked off her father's bedroom, den, and bathroom.

There was no place in the living room to store any paperwork, but Maggie began pulling out furniture and looking anyway. The boxes were in the way now that she decided she needed to finish pulling out the furniture and vacuum once she looked at the layer of dust hiding behind everything. She spent the next hour taking the boxes into the kitchen and lining them up along the wall. It was out of the traffic path, and she wasn't going to have to move them again until she either decided to burn it all or take it with her when she left. Maggie tried not to think about leaving, so she got back to work and spent all her energy into cleaning the living room.

As she completed placing the furniture back, she heard her phone ring. She grabbed it and noted it was Robert. "Robert! Thank heavens. We have a problem."

"You sound out of breath. What is going on out there?"

"Sorry. I was just cleaning the living room and had just pushed the furniture back. Let me sit down here." Maggie flopped on the couch and was pleased no puffs of dirt popped up. "Okay. This is the deal." Maggie started by telling Robert about all the farmers who leased the land and their conversations with Gary Johnson trying to sell land he didn't own. She relayed about having two payments from the leases, so they had half the money they needed for the back taxes. Then she explained about coming home and finding someone skulking around the house and yard and how she found the tracks that morning and was waiting for a deputy to arrive.

Robert listened throughout her story and tried to not interrupt Maggie as she was talking a mile a minute. "All right, sis. Hang on. I have no idea why someone would be wandering around there in the dark, but let the deputy handle it. You still have the shotgun by the front door?"

"Absolutely."

"I guess that's a good thing, then, for now. But be careful. Now. Let me tell you what I know on our end. Jack has been amazing. His contacts have got a lead on what this Johnson fellow is up to. It is an alias, but that's all I'm going to mention right now. Our lawyer is on it and has been making the contacts we need to get this guy. I'm still not sure where the banker plays into this, but the money has to flow somewhere, and by the sounds of this banker, even Dad didn't trust him. We'll keep working on the legal angles from here. No luck finding where the money went?"

"None. I'm cleaning room by room and haven't had any luck. No paper trail, and I've looked through the files twice since I pulled them out of the drawer. I have everything boxed up and stacked against the long kitchen wall. I was using the living room, but I needed see if there was anything behind the furniture in there. It's just been a dead end everywhere I look. I'll finish up the house this next week and then start on what's left of the outbuildings. The place looks so different without the barn and the chicken coop. I'm just glad I still have a solid shed for the car."

They talked awhile longer, and Robert agreed that Maggie should put the money in the same bank and adjust the loan request. Since they paid off the old debts and all they needed was half the amount originally requested for the taxes, she might have half a chance to get the loan. Maggie expressed doubt but agreed to try. She couldn't put Joe's check in until Monday afternoon anyway, so she had plenty of time to get the paperwork ready.

As she was finishing up her conversation with Robert, the deputy drove in. She went out to meet him and walked him over to the tracks. "Hard-soled shoe? Who in their right mind wears those out here?" Maggie had to agree it was certainly unusual. They followed the path, and she showed him the car tracks. She explained while they walked how she noticed something moving in the dark last night so she then checked that morning after she got up. Maggie left the deputy taking pictures and making notes and walked back to the house. She decided to sit out under her favorite tree and smiled as she remembered Luke asking about it. "I'll probably see him at church tomorrow." She sat daydreaming until the deputy walked back over and asked a few more questions before leaving.

"Next time, call us when you think you see something. Now that you know there really was someone out here, it will pay to be diligent." He pointed to the tarps. "The house isn't that secure, you know." Maggie agreed and really hoped to not see anyone again. All she could think about was the hard-soled shoe and Gary Johnson. It had to be him. Who else would be out here? That same chill went up her spine again.

CHAPTER 7

Maggie drove to town and went directly to the bank on Monday afternoon. She wasn't going to even ask to see the banker as she knew he would let her sit there and wait like the last time. She walked over and talked to the receptionist briefly about leaving her file for the banker, then strode to the teller and deposited the two checks into her account. As she was leaving, Mr. Jensen came out of his office when he realized Maggie was going to drop things off and leave.

"Leaving without talking to me, Maggie?"

"I left everything with the front office girl. I have amended my request for funds, and everything you need should be in the folder."

"I see. Well, let's take a quick look at it." He walked over and picked up the folder and began to go back to his office. Maggie remained close to the door. When Mr. Jensen noticed she wasn't following him, he turned back around. "You're not coming to my office?"

"I think not, Mr. Jensen. I need to go, and you can review that at your leisure. I won't take up any more of your time." With that, Maggie left the bank with Mr. Jensen's mouth gaping open and the receptionist grinning behind her hand.

Maggie picked up a few groceries on her way out of town and headed for home. She didn't want to run into anyone else today. Just going to the bank had irritated her. As she drove home, she thought about someone walking around her yard and not having any way to protect herself. Maggie picked up her phone and called Luke. It went directly to voice mail.

"Hi. This is Maggie. I have a job for you. Could you stop out at the house when you're free? I need a couple of things done right away and need either you or your dad, or maybe both of you. Thanks."

Maggie was just pulling into the drive when Luke called her back.

"I'll be there early this evening. What's up?"

"I'll explain when you get here. I've got a situation on my hands."

"Sounds ominous. I'll be there right after I get cleaned up and get a bite to eat."

"See you then."

Maggie fussed and fumed the rest of the afternoon. She felt aggravated and out of sorts. Maggie tried to shake off the feeling as she didn't want to take her problems out on Luke. She fixed a light supper and went outside to wait Luke's arrival. Luke called to let her know he was on the way, so she prepared some ice tea and grabbed an extra chair and a little table to sit the glasses on. When Luke arrived, he smiled when he saw her sitting under the elm tree.

"I think this is becoming a habit." Luke sat down and looked out across the yard. "You're right. This is a great place to sit."

Maggie smiled back and handed him a bowl of ice cream. "I know. I'll miss this view when I have to move."

Luke frowned at her. "Are you giving up?"

"I don't know. I'm feeling sorry for myself today, and this past month has been so trying. Not even my students on a bad day have made me feel this much stress."

Luke chuckled at the comparison. "That bad, huh?"

"You have no idea!"

They sat in a comfortable silence for a few minutes before Maggie finally decided to discuss why she brought Luke out to the farm.

"I had a visitor Friday night, but he didn't want me to know he was here."

"What are you talking about?"

Maggie explained about seeing someone sneaking around the yard and finding the tracks the next day. "I called the sheriff's office, and a deputy came out. There won't be much they can do at this point as we can't prove who was here."

"But you think it was that Johnson guy."

"Yeah."

"So why did you call me out here exactly?"

"First of all, I need you to help me change out the bulb that is burnt out in the yard light. I can't reach it. Then I want you to arrange for your father to come over and close up the house properly. I'm not safe with a just a tarp if someone tries to get in. I'll pay both of you, of course. I have some money in the bank now."

"I can get the light. I have an extension ladder on the truck. Do you have a bulb?"

"In the shop. We can talk while we walk out there."

Maggie explained that she decided her safety was more important right now than the money, so she needed to take care of things immediately. She reached to a shelf and retrieved the lightbulb, and they walked over to the truck. Luke got his ladder and set it up and took the bulb. In a couple of minutes, the bulb was changed and the ladder back on the truck.

"That seemed way too simple. I don't know what happened to our extension ladder. Maybe it was blown away in the storm."

"No problem. Now let me call my father, and you can discuss things with him." Luke dialed his father up, and after explaining that Maggie needed some help right away, he handed the phone over to her. Maggie explained that she needed a way to seal up the house for safety reasons, and if he could get a group together quickly, she would appreciate it. Seth said he would be by the following day to look at the house again and give her an estimate on cost and a time frame. She thanked him and handed the phone back to Luke. They talked briefly before hanging up.

"Do you need any other repairs tonight?"

"No, but if you know someone that has a good watchdog, I could certainly use one. Besides, I'd been thinking about getting one anyway since I'm out here by myself. The dog has to work for a living, though. I want one that will actually bark at an intruder."

Luke smiled. "I know exactly who to call. I have an old friend that trains dogs. I'll give him a buzz." Fifteen minutes later, Maggie had a date with a dog trainer the first of next week. Luke offered to drive her out to his place, and she thought that would be a great idea.

"How about sitting with me for a bit?"

"I'd love to." They both sat down under the elm and slowly sipped their tea. As night fell, the yard light came on and offered a soft glow to the yard.

"I feel safer with the yard light on."

"You know, I was thinking the same thing. Maggie, I'm worried about you staying out here by yourself. Especially with just a tarp between you and someone intent on getting into the house."

"Don't worry, Luke. I have a .410, and I'm not afraid to use it."

"Tough guy, huh? Remind me not to sneak up on you again."

They both laughed, and Luke reached over to hold Maggie's hand. "Thanks for calling me to help you. Call me anytime, you hear?"

Maggie smiled at Luke and squeezed his hand. "I will, Luke. I promise."

The following day, Seth arrived with two of his sons. They both looked remarkably like their father, and she thought Luke must take after his mother. Seth and his sons looked at the damage once again and told Maggie they would be back in the next couple of days to work on the house. They thought that with a group they could have it taken care of by the end of the week if they didn't find any added structural problems. Seth explained the labor charge and told her he had a surprise for her on the supplies but wouldn't give her a clue. "You will just have to wait and see, young lady. Wait and see." Seth smiled, and he and his boys got back into the truck to leave.

Wednesday arrived, and Maggie knew that sometime that day her loan would be reviewed. She didn't know how soon she would find out anything, but she didn't count on getting the funds. Maggie hoped Robert and Jack were having better luck. They were on the countdown, and July had run out. August meant only four weeks left.

By Friday, Maggie hadn't heard from the banker. She decided to not call and check as in her heart she knew there wouldn't be any loan. Seth and his crew came on Wednesday afternoon to drop off supplies and equipment. Seth explained that much of the lumber was actually from the trees that they had cleaned up from her yard. There was a lot of good wood, and Seth owned a small mill and kiln. Maggie was surprised and touched that Seth spent the time curing wood to use on her house. It made the repair work more special to her.

The crew returned on Thursday morning early and tore off the tarps and began to repair the storm damage. Maggie sat under the tree and watched them work steadily throughout the morning. The smell of fresh lumber often wafted over the breeze. Maggie was thinking she should prepare the crew something cold to drink when a couple of vehicles drove into the yard and women piled out and began to set up for a meal and drinks for the crew. Maggie walked over as she watched them put things together quickly and efficiently. She introduced herself to the oldest woman and found out it was Luke's mother. As Maggie had thought, Luke looked a lot like her. She excused herself to go into the house and prepare her own lunch. Maggie watched as the men were called over for their meal and prayed before being served. They took their plates and sat under the old elm, cooling off and resting for an hour before returning to work. The women packed everything back up and left. Maggie decided she would go to the basement and get out of everyone's way. The men were in and out of the house, and there was a lot of noise from hammers and saws. She retrieved her latest book and sat on the couch. Before long, the noise escaped to the background as she became involved in her story.

By Friday, the repair crew had not only repaired the house; they had enough lumber left to build her a small deck off the back door. Seth told her that when he finished curing the rest of the lumber, he would return and build an overhang to provide shelter from the sun and rain. She took Seth's hand and shook it. "You don't know how much this means to me." Seth handed Maggie the key to the back door.

"Just lock up behind you. Luke told us you had an uninvited visitor the other night."

"I will, Seth. Bring me a bill next week so I can get you paid."

Seth finished loading up a few tools and headed out. Maggie waved as they left. She held the key in her hand. *Finally. A lock for the back door.*

With the house finally buttoned up, the air conditioner didn't have to work overtime to cool the kitchen off. Maggie found herself sleeping well again now that she didn't worry about someone working their way through tarps. Her appointment with the dog trainer was on Tuesday afternoon. She was looking forward to it, not only because she would be getting a dog, but she would get to be with Luke.

Maggie spent the weekend cleaning up the dust created by the rebuilding. She did manage to go to church and sat with Luke once again. She was enjoying the services and thought that if she ended up staying in the area, she would think about joining a Sunday school class. On Monday, Maggie sat down and worked on a resume for the local school system. It was too late in the year for a permanent position, but she could certainly offer herself as a substitute teacher. If she didn't stay, it wouldn't affect anyone but herself. Maggie finished up the resume and sent it off to the school district. After the storm took her phone lines out, she had shut the phone service off but asked to have Internet service only. It wasn't fast, but it was good enough to get and send an occasional e-mail.

Maggie looked around Tuesday morning and decided the cleanup from the building project was completed. She needed to get back to looking for clues to her dad's money but was running out of places to look. The whole upstairs was now clean. Maggie decided to peek into the attic. To her knowledge, nothing was ever stored there. She found a step ladder and put it just below the trapdoor. Maggie carefully lifted an edge and was greeted by heat and insulation. She had brought a flashlight with her, and once she was able to get past falling insulation, she quickly stuck her head through the opening and looked around. The only thing she saw was insulation, wiring, and the stack pipes going through the roof. She quickly closed the door and got off the ladder. Maggie looked at the floor and saw the mess she made. She quickly put the ladder away and got out the trusty vacuum to clean up yet another mess.

Maggie stood with her hands on her hips. *I guess my next move is to go downstairs.* She looked at the clock and realized Luke would be there after lunch to pick her up. Instead of spending any more time searching, she took a quick shower to get rid of the insulation in her hair and then fixed a quick lunch. As she was rinsing her dishes, Luke drove in and stood looking at the house. Maggie made sure both doors were securely locked and came out to greet him.

"Your father did a nice job."

"He sure did. Do you feel better now?"

"Absolutely, but I'll feel a lot better if I get a good watchdog out here. We always had one growing up, and I didn't realize how much I missed not only the companionship but the noise they make when someone drives in."

"Well, let's go see what we can find for you."

The two hopped into the truck and went to Luke's friend, Jeff. Jeff was a retired police officer and had a canine dog when he was working. He enjoyed the dog so much that he spent his retirement training dogs for protecting homes. Luke introduced the two, and Jeff immediately brought her toward the kennels and explained how she would need to stand back as they walked along the kennels and decide on which one looked promising to her, one that she thought she could handle, and one that looked like he would like her back. Jeff explained that not only must she consider the dog, but the dog must consider her.

Luke and Maggie followed Jeff as he began the short walk along the kennels. Jeff had Maggie take the lead and told her to talk to each one. There were a dozen kennels, and as Maggie came to the second to the last one, she stopped. The German shepherd sat looking at her, and Maggie looked back and talked softly to him.

"That's King. I've had him for eight months, and he has never sat like that for anyone except me. Let me get him out, Maggie."

"Yes, do. I think it was love at first sight. Look at the color of his eyes! And the color of his coat is beautiful!"

Jeff unlocked the kennel and clipped on a leash. He led King out and over to Maggie.

"Hold your hand out for him to sniff." Maggie did as she was told, and King sniffed her hand and then licked it. "He is giving you permission to pet him."

Maggie reached over and slowly began petting the dog. She sat down in front of the dog, and King lay down in front of her and rolled on his back.

Jeff took one look at the dog and Maggie, then at Luke. "I think you have a winner."

Maggie laughed quietly and continued to pet the dog and love him up. "You're such a good dog, King. Want to go home with me?" King jumped up and climbed onto Maggie's lap.

Jeff and Luke were quite surprised at the dog's response. "I think that's a yes. Let me show you what you need to do once you get home with him."

Jeff led Maggie and King through a series of workouts. She needed to know how to show him the farm boundaries and several commands that the dog had been taught. When Jeff was sure that Maggie had all the commands down, he prepared the paperwork for her.

"I hope you two get along once you get home, but I don't think that is going to be a problem." Jeff laughed at how the two were connecting. "Now he's used to being outside, so just make sure he has a place to get out of the weather. Since you want a watchdog, you don't want him inside anyway, because that is too late to alert you if someone attempts to sneak up on you in the middle of the night."

"I understand. The shop is always open, so I can put an old blanket or something out there for him."

"Well, you're set then. Take him home and show him his boundaries before it gets too late."

Maggie and Luke loaded the dog into the back of the truck and headed for the farm. Jeff lent them a kennel for transport, and Luke would return it the following day. Maggie talked all the way home about the dog and how much fun she had working with him. When they got to the farm, she hooked the leash on him, and Luke walked with them around the yard boundaries. It took a little while as the dog continually sniffed at trees and bushes. As they rounded the house, Maggie retrieved a couple of blankets and pillows she had tossed out and walked them to the shop. She unclipped the leash, and Luke threw the pillows and blankets on the floor. Maggie told King to lie down, and the dog did as he was told. "Good dog." She reached into her pocket and retrieved the snack that Jeff had given her to help train King. She threw it to him and looked over at Luke. "I'm going to have to get some food."

Luke grinned. "I'll be right back." Maggie gave him a questioning look but went on ahead and found a couple of tins she could use for food and water. She walked to a hydrant and filled the water bowl. By then Luke had returned with a twenty-pound bag of dog food. "Where did that come from?"

"Well, I figured you wouldn't have time to shop for anything, so I picked some up before I came to get you."

"You're so thoughtful!" Maggie had him pour some in the food tin she had placed. King sniffed at it but continued to lie on the blanket. "Well, I guess we shall leave him be and see if he stays or runs off."

They walked hand in hand on the way to the truck. "You want to stay for supper? I don't want to leave since I just got the dog here."

"Sure. I'd be happy to hang around. Want some help?"

"Well, there isn't that much room to work in the kitchen, but you could fix up the salads, and I can throw on some spaghetti."

"I think that sounds delicious."

Once supper was over, Maggie walked Luke out to the truck. They noticed King out in the yard sniffing around, but he didn't go far. If someone drove by, he immediately stopped and watched until the vehicle was long gone, then went back to his hunting. Luke felt that the dog was probably Maggie's best investment so far and told her that.

"Well, that and fixing the house. Now I can lock both doors when I'm gone."

"Speaking of which, I need to take off. I have an early job to get to tomorrow. Thanks so much for supper."

"It's the least I could do for you taking me over to Jeff's."

"I just wanted the dog to know I was safe so he wouldn't attack me if I snuck up on you again."

"Oh, you!" Maggie swatted at Luke's arm. "You're never going to let me live that down, are you?"

Luke laughed. "Nope!"

Maggie watched him leave, and King came over and stood by her side. She stood there, petting him long after Luke left. *It's just you and me, King. You do your job, and I'll keep you in all the kibbles you can eat!*

The following morning, Maggie was greeted by a friendly dog bark. She had looked out the window, and King had welcomed her. She laughed and after breakfast went out to make sure there was still food and gave him fresh water. The bedding looked as if the dog had made himself comfortable in the night. She hadn't gotten the mail for a few days, and as she walked to the mailbox, the dog stayed right with her. On the walk back, Maggie looked at the mail and saw an envelope from the bank. She tore it open and read the denial for a loan. Maggie groaned, and the dog leaned close to her leg. She reached down and patted the dog and reassured him she was okay. *I better ask Joe and Sheila who they use as a banker.*

It had been a few days since she had talked to Robert, so she thought with the bank refusal, she better notify him. Robert was in his office when she called and was patched directly through. Maggie explained the letter, and Robert told her to go to another bank and see about a short-term loan and they could fax the paperwork to him for his signature. Maggie had kept a copy of everything she had given to her father's bank, so she planned to call Sheila as soon as she got off the phone. Robert told her they hadn't gotten any further information for about Gary Johnson, but the lawyer assured Robert that things were moving quickly, and the state and federal agencies were quite interested in the case. Maggie told Robert she had spent some money to fix the house up and get a dog to provide her with some extra safety, and Robert felt better now that she could lock both doors.

"I'll come out if they can take those guys down. I don't want to miss the excitement."

"Robert! I didn't know you had it in you!"

Robert chuckled. "No one messes with the Chesneys!"

As soon as Maggie hung up, she called Sheila. She gave her the name of the bank and said to wait until Joe had called their loan officer as he was a friend of theirs. Sheila said she would have the bank call her and let her know when to come in. She thanked her good friend and then went on to ask about the kids. Maggie received a call late that day from Joe's bank, and they arranged a meeting for the following afternoon. She sat down and reviewed all the paperwork and had it ready to take with her. She sat back and smiled. There wasn't much time left, but she thought that maybe this bank would at least treat her well. Maggie balanced the checkbook and decided she would close out her current account and open one at the new bank even if she didn't get the loan, and that made her feel better just thinking about it.

The heat wave was continuing as summer drug on, but it was typical of Nebraska weather. An occasional shower would pop up in the late afternoon, but there hadn't been any bad storms since the home place was torn up. The humidity was high as Maggie drove to the bank to close out her account. She was greeted warmly by the receptionist and teller, but Mr. Jensen stayed in his office. Maggie quietly asked to close the account and get a cashier's check for the balance. All of the checks she had written had been canceled. It wasn't until she was almost out the door that Mr. Jensen stopped her.

"Maggie, I thought you would want to see me about the loan."

"Why? You gave me your answer before you had your meeting."

"I tried to make it happen. Honest."

"It doesn't matter now, does it? By the way, I just closed out my account. I won't need your services any longer."

Mr. Jensen blustered a bit. "Now, now. You don't need to go do that. You father had his account here for years."

"Mr. Jensen, you have made it perfectly clear from the onset that you did not appreciate my business. Good-bye." At that, she pivoted out the doors and left Mr. Jensen glaring at her.

Maggie headed off to Ogallala to Joe's bank. She made it a few minutes before her appointment but was shown in promptly upon announcing her arrival. After much discussion about needing enough to cover half of the taxes and money for repairs that needed to be done since the storm, she pulled out her cashier's check from the closed account. "I plan to open an account here, and I would be happy to use a section of ground as collateral for the rest of the money I need to take care of the taxes."

The banker reviewed the papers in front of him. "I'll need Robert's signature, of course, but I think we can do business. Let's see. Yes, you have Robert's phone and fax number right here. Let me give him a call." The banker proceeded to call Robert, and thankfully, he was in the office. The banker put the phone on speaker, and they held a conversation about loan terms and collateral. After he hung the phone up, the banker looked at Maggie. "I think we can do business with you. It's going to take about a week or so to get the papers together. I appreciate you providing the information on the section you wish to use for the loan, but I think we can hold that down to a half section. Even though no one is buying land, it still holds its value. A quarter would probably be enough, but the bank examiners would be happier with two quarters." The banker smiled at Maggie, and she couldn't help but smile back.

"You don't know how happy that makes me that we won't lose the farm."

"I knew your dad. He was an honest man. I'd hate for you kids to lose it over his lapse in judgment in his last couple of years."

Maggie stood. "It truly means the world to me. Thank you so much." They shook hands, and Maggie felt the worry of the world falling off her shoulders. She was directed to someone who would help her open a new account, and she kept smiling as she signed papers.

The next few days were spent looking and cleaning every nook and cranny she could find in the house. She even pulled down all the bookshelves and checked every book before putting them back on the shelf. Maggie attended church again with Luke but again returned home to continue cleaning and searching once the service was over. By that following Thursday, she had finished cleaning the house and decided it was time to take her search to the outbuildings. *At least I don't have to clean them!*

She walked to the shop, and King followed her. Maggie began searching along one wall, and King lay on his bed, watching. As she continued to dig through each drawer and look behind the workbenches, King began to growl and then bark. Maggie stopped and watched as King ran out of the shop and head for the house. She slowly walked out of the shop and watched King bark at a car that drove up the lane and park in front of the house. King stood outside the driver's door and continued bark and growl. The driver sat in the car and kept looking at the house. Maggie walked closer to the car and realized it was Gary Johnson. She stood by King and commanded him to sit and be quiet. King quickly obeyed but kept his eyes on the car. Gary slowly rolled his window down partway.

"Can you call off the dog so I can get out?"

"What do you want?"

"I need to talk to you."

"I repeat, what do you want?" She felt the dog tense as Maggie raised her voice.

"Listen. When are you leaving?"

"I don't know what you're talking about, Gary."

"Moving. Packing up. When are you leaving? What's so hard to understand about that?" Gary got out of the car carefully trying to stay away from the dog. Maggie kept a hand on King's head. Gary walked to the house and started to go in.

"What do you think you are doing? You can't go into my house!"

Gary opened the front door and walked in. Seeing the boxes sitting on the kitchen floor, he headed straight for them. Maggie was right behind him but left the dog outside the door.

"What do you think you are doing?"

"You can't have these files. I need them." Gary ignored Maggie and began to toss papers to the side as he was searching for something.

"What are you doing?" Maggie yelled. She picked up her phone and called 911. "Send someone immediately. I have an intruder." Maggie stayed connected to the dispatcher as she watched Gary knock boxes over, searching. "I don't know what you're looking for, but you need to leave right now!"

"You have to give me those files right now! They're mine, I tell you. Mine!" Gary had a wild look to his eyes.

Maggie realized Gary wasn't going to leave. She left her phone sitting on the end table just outside the kitchen doorway and quickly reached for the .410. She checked to make sure there were still shells in it, slapped the gun together, and took off the safety. Maggie raised the gun and spoke loudly so the dispatcher could hear her. "Gary, I have a shotgun pointed at you right now, so if you know what is good for you, you will leave the house immediately. And I'm not going to call off the dog, so you better hightail it to your car."

Gary stopped and looked at her coldly. "You wouldn't dare."

"I have the dispatcher listening in. If there is one thing you better understand, I'm a pretty decent shot. At this range, there will no issue with me missing you. Do you want to take that chance?" Maggie put her shoulder into the stock and, keeping her finger off the trigger, pointed the gun directly at Gary. "You have ten seconds to leave, or I pull the trigger. It's your decision." Maggie proceeded to start counting down from ten. As she reached four, she made a point of looking down the sight. On three, Gary took off running out the door and headed for his car, the dog growling and grabbing his pant leg and pulling on it. He managed to get loose and jump in the car. King jumped on the side of the car and tried to get in the partially open window as Gary fumbled his keys before getting the car started. Maggie stood at the front door aiming the gun at his car. Gary got his car started and took off down the lane, King chasing him to the road. Maggie went back into the house and picked up her phone.

"He left. Do you still have someone on their way?"

"I sure do, Maggie. Hold on." The dispatcher paused for a bit. "In fact, it sounds like they stopped him about one mile from your place. The deputy was pretty close."

"Thank you." Maggie dropped the phone and sat on the couch. She was shaking like a leaf. Maggie managed to put the safety on the gun and laid it on the floor. She didn't know how long she sat there trying to get her emotions under control before she heard King barking again. Maggie walked to the door and saw a deputy pulling in. She walked outside and again commanded King to sit. King sat leaning next to Maggie, and she reached down to stroke his head. It comforted Maggie as much as King enjoyed it.

"I see you got a dog since I was last here. Looks like a good one."

Maggie reached out and shook the deputy's hand. Jeff had taught her that King would understand that it was a friend if she shook someone's hand. King relaxed against her.

"Do you want to press charges?"

"Yes, I do. Come on in, and I'll show you what he did."

Maggie brought the deputy in and showed him the mess Gary had made of the files and how he was looking for something specific. The deputy stated he was glad she had left the phone connected to the dispatcher because it recorded what was going on and what was said. The deputy asked to see her shotgun, and Maggie pointed it out on the floor.

"I have the safety on. When I found it in the pantry, I put it behind the door. Who knew I would actually need it?" Maggie sat back down and watched the deputy check the gun over.

"A little bulky for home safety, but I guess it did the job."

"Yea, and Gary's right. I probably couldn't have pulled the trigger and hit him. I would have shot a hole in the ceiling or at the wall as a scare tactic, though."

"So you don't know what he was looking for?"

"No. I've looked through those files more than once, and I can't imagine there being anything in there that would pertain to him. They are just old bank statements and bills. Typical household stuff. I planned on burning it all eventually."

The deputy took several pictures of the mess Gary had made and a couple of the shotgun. He asked Maggie to stop by the station the next day after she calmed down to make her statement and press charges.

"I'm going to need a restraining order on him too if he bails out. I don't want him to come near me."

"I'm sure we can arrange that. Just stop by, and we can get all that done at the same time."

After the deputy left, Maggie sat on the step, holding the dog and petting him. King sat by her side, and they both finally relaxed. *Well, King. I have a mess to clean up.* Maggie went back into the house and looked closely at every piece of paper she picked up before stuffing it back into a box. Gary had knocked three of the boxes completely over, and a fourth one was a mess. She decided to sort as she went through them. All of the old utility and doctor bills were thrown in a box by themselves. Anything that had to do with the taxes or farm related she put in another box. She worked well into the supper hour before quitting. She still couldn't figure out what Gary would want out of those papers, but she was too tired to care at this point.

Maggie checked on King and made sure there were food and water. It was still unbearably hot out that evening, so she made short work of her chores. She fixed a sandwich for supper and went to bed early. It was an exhausting day and figured she would call Robert in the morning to let him know what had happened.

CHAPTER 8

The following morning, Maggie called Robert as soon as she got up. After detailing the episode with Gary and the sheriff's office, Robert had become agitated.

"What is your next step, sis? I'm not comfortable with everything you have had to put up with these last few weeks."

"Well, I'm headed to Ogallala to give my statement and try to get a restraining order while I'm there."

"When is the bank loan going to be ready?"

"I haven't heard yet, but I can check while I'm in town. Why?"

"I'm going to take a couple of weeks of vacation and come home. I'll leave the family here for now. Call me when you find out about the paperwork, and I'll get a flight out."

"Are you sure you can take the time?"

"Things have slowed down, and I can have Jack watch the projects for me. He knows what is going on, and after I let him know the latest, he'll probably be taking me to the airport himself."

"I could use the help around here. You can help me figure out what Dad did with his money."

"I'm as worried about that as you are, but with someone else at the house, it will deter people from coming out and scaring you, I think. Give me a call later, and I'll get the plane tickets."

"That will be great. Talk to you soon."

Maggie headed to town and spent an hour and half giving her statement and working on the restraining order. Her neck muscles were screaming from being so tight from the stress. Gary was going to be arraigned later that day and would probably be let loose without bail. She hoped the restraining order would be in effect by then. The deputy said they were taking it to the judge that morning and thought it would be addressed during the hearing.

She drove over to the bank and parked and sat in the car rolling her shoulders, trying to loosen them up before walking into the bank. When she felt a little more relaxed, Maggie went in and asked to see the banker. She found he was with a client, so she left her number to have him call as soon as possible. As she walked back to the car, Maggie decided to stop and get a bite to eat somewhere. She looked down and saw she needed gas too. She sighed and drove to the nearest gas station. After filling the tank, she walked in and found a couple of donuts and got a cup of coffee to go with it and sat in a booth watching traffic while she ate.

Maggie had been daydreaming about Luke and was startled when her phone rang. The banker let her know when the loan would be ready and was happy to know Robert would be coming to sign the papers instead of him faxing them. "It's just easier, you know, and he and I were in the same class in school. It will be good to see him again." Maggie called Robert and let him know. He was going to fly into North Platte and would call her back when to pick him up.

"Do you think you can stay in Dad's room? That way you can have a bathroom to yourself."

"Sure. It will be weird the first night, but that's all right."

"Great. I'll make up the bed and get a fan going to cool things off. Your room in the basement is mostly clean but seriously needs a makeover." They both laughed at the teenager look of the room and decided he could throw out his old stuff since she didn't want to touch it.

Maggie found some treats and doggie dishes at the farm store, then picked up some groceries and headed for home. She needed to finish searching the shop today. Maggie found a variety of antique tools that she sorted through and put in its own place on the workbench. She would have Robert look at things when he got there and see if she should auction the contents of the outbuildings. It seemed a shame to let everything sit around and not be used by someone. Maggie made up a toolbox of her own and organized the pegboard with the box end wrenches. Although she swore she wasn't going to clean the outbuildings, she was sure making a dent in this one. She took a lot of trash to the barrel and made a recycle box for oil and paint cans. King continued to watch her from his bed and seemed content, his ears always moving as if listening for visitors.

Maggie's donuts had worn off hours ago. She was filthy from working in the shop and decided to call it a day. Robert was flying in on Wednesday, and their appointment at the bank was the following day. They would make the deadline for paying the taxes in plenty of time. Maggie gave King fresh water and hit the shower. Just as she was sitting down to her supper, Luke called.

"I just heard that Gary Johnson was arrested for breaking in to your place. Is that true?"

"Yes, it is." Maggie sighed and then repeated what had happened.

"Why didn't you call me? I could have come out to be with you after that."

"I didn't think about it. I was pretty shook up. I didn't even call my brother until the following morning."

"I see. Maggie, you know I can be there in fifteen minutes if you need me."

"Thank you, Luke. I really hate to impose. It happened so fast, and then I collapsed in bed that evening. I'm all right. And Robert is arriving on Wednesday to help me finish up the sorting and going to the bank. We got the loan, and we'll get those taxes paid yet."

"I'm glad you won't be alone then."

"Listen, Luke. I just sat down to my supper, so I better eat. Thanks for calling."

"Sure. Sure. Take care, Maggie."

Maggie went back to her meal and opened up her laptop to check her e-mails.

Luke looked at the phone after hanging up. He thought he was making progress with their relationship, but she didn't seem very interested in him, and he didn't know what to think about it. She had been going through a lot, so maybe this wasn't the right time. Luke shrugged and went off to fix his own supper.

Seth showed up the following day, and he and his boys built the structure over the deck to provide shade and protection from the rain. It only took them a couple of hours, and she enjoyed watching it go up. She settled the bill with him afterward and added a little extra to help pay for the use of his kiln. "Thank you so much, Seth. I appreciate you and your family so much. I hope we can always be there for each other over the years."

"I do too, Maggie. Just call me if something else comes up."

"Believe me, I will."

Maggie finished the sorting in the shop and even looked up in the rafters. She decided she was done until Robert got home. There were two buildings left: the shed where the car was parked and one that looked like it was going to fall down. She hadn't even opened the door on that one. The granaries and silos were completely empty. She did poke her head in the pump house, but she never liked the place and closed the door quickly.

The following day, Maggie needed to be in North Platte by eleven; so she grabbed a quick bite, checked on King, and headed out. She sang along with the radio station and felt the happiest she had in a couple of months. Just knowing they would save the farm was enough for her at this point. Robert's flight was on time, and they stopped in town to get a bite to eat. As they were catching up, a man stopped by their table.

"Are you the Chesney kids?"

They looked up. Robert put his hand out. "And you are?"

The man shook Robert's hand. "Gabriel Canon. I am on the board at the bank. I assume you have your money now and things are going well?"

Maggie frowned she looked at him. "Which bank are you referring to, Mr. Canon?"

"I'm on the board at your bank and William Jensen was supposed to get the loan papers together for you." Maggie and Robert looked at each other. "I assume your silence to mean you never got the money?"

"Mr. Canon, Mr. Jensen never had any intention of loaning me anything. He told me that up front. Are you saying the board approved the loan?"

"Of course we did. Your father banked with us for years! What kind of nonsense is this?"

Maggie reached over and pulled the denial letter out of her purse. She had put it in there to take to the new bank in case she needed proof of denial and had never taken it back out. "As you can see, here is my denial letter. I also closed my account with the bank shortly after that."

"I see. I'm sorry to hear that. I believe the board and Mr. Jensen will be having another meeting."

Robert looked back up at him. "If I could ask you to sit with me a moment, I want to discuss something with you."

Mr. Canon sat down quickly. Robert reached over and put his hand on Mr. Canon's arm to bring him closer and quietly discussed the possibility of the bank examiners coming to check Mr. Jensen out due to his association with Mr. Johnson. "I don't want you to do anything right now. This will come to a head shortly. In fact, I believe he will be visited by someone next week. So you see, I want you to let it go until after the investigation gets completed. Can I expect you to keep this completely quiet until then?"

Mr. Canon looked appalled that the bank might be involved in a scheme to defraud customers but knew he was unable to do anything himself. "I won't say a thing, but you will keep me informed?"

"I don't think I'll have to. I think you will know exactly when things come down. There will be multiple people involved in things like this, and Mr. Jensen seems the type to be a bully to someone like Maggie, but when the chips fall, he will roll over on anyone involved to save himself."

They all talked quietly for a few more minutes, then left for their own destinations. Maggie and Robert were quiet most of the way home, lost in their own thoughts. As they neared the farm, she asked the all-important question.

"Do you think they will get everyone involved in this?"

"I hope so, Maggie. I doubt people will be quiet in order to save their own skin. It's nature to blame everyone else for their sins."

"True. I'll just be glad when this is over."

Maggie pulled into the drive, but King didn't meet her. "That's weird."

"What?"

"My dog. He didn't greet me."

"Maybe he's off snooping somewhere."

"Hmm. Maybe. Let's get you in the house. You'll be surprised at how clean it is. I don't know if you've ever seen it this clean!"

As Robert got out of the car, he looked at the new construction. "That looks great! I love the covered porch over the deck!"

"It is great. I haven't had a chance to use it yet, but we'll try it out later. Let's use the front door for now and get your suitcases dropped off in the bedroom. I even bought you new pillows."

They gathered up everything and headed up to the door. Maggie screamed. Robert dropped his bags and grabbed her. "What is it?"

"Look! There's blood all over!" Robert looked at the sidewalk and steps and then noticed blood in the yard. "Look at my door!" Robert looked up at the door and saw the lock was smashed. At first glance, you didn't see that the door wasn't completely closed.

"Call the sheriff's office right now, Maggie." Maggie grabbed her phone and dialed. It took her twice since she was shaking so much. Robert looked around and decided to follow the path of the blood while Maggie was talking to the dispatcher. After she hung up, she watched Robert. She was shaking so much she couldn't follow him. Robert walked on out to the shop and found King lying in a pool of blood. He was still alive, but barely. He turned and yelled at Maggie. "Call a vet! Your dog has been hurt!"

Maggie screamed and ran out to the shed and looked at King. She dropped down beside him and put his head on her lap and began bawling. "Who would do such a thing? Who?"

"We need a vet, Maggie."

"I don't know one! I haven't had him long enough to need one!"

"Who can I call?"

It took Maggie a few seconds. "Luke. Call Luke. The number is in the phone." She tossed her phone to Robert. He found Luke's number and called him. Luke agreed to get a vet out there immediately and said he would also be coming. "It's okay, sis. Luke will handle it. You stay with him, and I'll handle the deputies."

Within a half an hour, the place was teeming with activity. The vet and Luke showed up about the same time and took over for Maggie. She was covered with blood. Maggie went over and sat on a bench while the vet provided emergency care. Luke walked over to her. "I think he has the bleeding stopped, but he needs to take him in to the office to care for him."

"What happened to him? What happened?" Maggie sat there crying and rocking herself. Luke sat down and held her close.

"Someone shot him. Whoever broke into your house knew he was here and shot him."

"My god."

The vet came over and knelt down in front of Maggie. "Listen. He lost a lot of blood. I think the bullet may have missed his heart and lungs, but the blood loss is bad. I need to take him in and get him on the table to get the bullet out of there and patch him up. You can have Luke bring you in later. I'll be in the office until late. He can call me when you're on your way so I can unlock for you."

"Thanks. I'll be in after I clean up."

Luke and the vet loaded King up in the truck, and the vet headed out quickly. Luke took Maggie by the hands and led her over to the hydrant to wash some of the blood off both of them. He then walked her over to Robert, who explained that someone had indeed broken in and she would have to tell them what was taken. Maggie struggled up the stairs and walked into the house. The nice clean house was in shambles. The files were gone, and the furniture was in disarray. As she walked downstairs, it was also in as big a mess. She sat on the couch and began crying again. Robert sat down beside her.

"He is one sick guy. Shoots my dog and messes up my house."

Luke and the deputies stood by.

"Maggie, we've taken pictures of everything. When I was here the other day, I noticed how neat and tidy everything was, so I realize this isn't the normal state of things. We've probably got enough prints on things to nail Mr. Johnson to the wall."

"I don't know why he wanted those files. There was nothing in them. Nothing. Just old receipts. I went through them three times. I have no idea what he wanted."

"We have the sheriff himself and another deputy headed to his place to see what we can find out. The restraining order went through, and he knew he wasn't supposed to be out here. That is just another strike against him."

Maggie was exhausted from crying. "I can't catch a break. Just as things start to look better, something else happens. The house can be put back together, but my dog is another matter. He may have killed my dog."

"We'll find the gun and take care of that matter too. If it looks like just the files are gone, we'll get out of here and help the sheriff out. Is there anyone else you think we should check out?"

"Who picked him up from jail?"

"Mr. Jensen, the banker."

Robert replied. "You better check him out too. I've got bank examiners on the way, and the real estate licensing board is checking out Mr. Johnson. By the way, now that you have prints, you might want to find out who he really is. There is no record of a Gary Johnson."

"Robert, I believe you and I better have a conversation." Robert got up and followed the deputy out of the house, and Robert relayed the story to the deputy.

Luke sat down beside Maggie. "If you are ready, how about we go see King?"

Maggie looked at her clothes. "I better clean up first. You can use the bathroom upstairs and wash up. I'll use the bathroom down here, change, and then I'll meet you out front."

"Okay. I'll see you in a little bit." Luke hugged her close for a minute before letting her go and slowly walked up the stairs.

Maggie walked to the bathroom and saw she had blood everywhere, even in her hair. She decided to grab a quick shower, and even then, she wasn't sure she felt clean. Maggie quickly dried her hair and met everyone out front after about twenty minutes.

Robert came over. "I'm going to stay here and put the place to rights while Luke runs you to the vet. The deputy will get a report from the vet tomorrow on his findings. And, Maggie? It's going to be all right."

Maggie nodded, and Luke led her over to his truck and headed off to see King. Robert finished his conversation with the deputy and was just clearing up loose ends when the radio crackled with the report that Gary Johnson was on the run and the sheriff was on his tail.

The deputy excused himself and took off. The forensic team had already left, and Robert stood there looking around. He noticed where the barn and chicken coop used to be and walked down to the shed where the truck sat. Robert patted it, then walked over to the trunk that Maggie had told him about. He picked it up and hefted it back to the house, sat it inside the back door, then went to work, setting the house back in order. He called his wife and Jack later to let them know the newest developments.

Luke called the vet to let him know they were on the way. When they arrived, they were taken back to the room King was being held. "The bullet wasn't hard to find, and it did minimal damage because it was a small caliber, but he bled a lot. I got that stopped, and now we need to let him rest. I have him sedated, and he'll be out for the night. You can stay for a while, but then I'm going to move him to another room and get him settled for the night."

"Thanks, Doc." Luke shook his hand as the vet walked out of the room.

Maggie stood by King's side and continually smoothed his head and talked quietly to him. She looked up at Luke. "He was such a good dog. We hit it off so quickly just like it was meant to be. I never knew I could feel like this about an animal. The ones we had growing up were good dogs, but I was never attached to any of them like King."

Luke walked over and held Maggie close as she kept talking to the King. The vet finally came in and checked him out once again. "I think I need to settle him in. He's stable, and he won't know anything until at least midmorning. You can come back tomorrow and see him. King won't be able to go home for a few days as I'll have to keep him partially sedated and provide a little pain relief."

"Thank you, Doctor. I appreciate everything you've done to save him."

"Call me Hank." Maggie smiled and shook his hand.

"All right, Hank. I'll see you tomorrow. Take good care of my friend."

Luke walked Maggie out and helped her into the truck. After he got in, he sat for a bit before turning to her. "Maggie, I want to be there for you. Can I come get you tomorrow?"

"I'm sorry, Luke. I have to go to the bank first thing in the morning with Robert, and then we need to pay the taxes. I can call you after that and meet you later if you want."

"I'll take what I can get. This is a tough time, and I want to be there for you."

"Luke, I appreciate your friendship. After all this is behind me, I'd like to see where this goes."

Luke smiled. "That's all I ask. Just give me a chance."

Maggie couldn't help but smile back at him. She reached over and held his hand as they drove back to the farm. Luke walked her into the house, and they were both surprised at how fast Robert had put the house to rights again. Luke looked at the lock on the door.

"I'll be out tomorrow morning sometime and fix the door. I think I can fix it so no one will ever break in again. You have the back-door keys, right?"

"Yea."

"You won't be able to get in the front door once I change the locks. I'll leave the new keys on the table. Good luck at the bank tomorrow."

"Thanks, Luke."

Maggie turned and looked at the place. "I can't believe you got this back together already."

"It looks worse than it was. I just needed to put things back where they belonged. He didn't break anything except the door lock, and I'll put something against the door for the night."

"I'm going to bed. Once we get our business done tomorrow, I'm supposed to call Luke, and he'll meet me at the vets to check on King."

"Is he going to make it?"

"The vet thinks so. Right now he is sedated. He got the bullet out, and the bleeding stopped."

"Good. You want a bite to eat before you head off to bed? I made up a couple of sandwiches while you were gone and thought we could warm up some soup."

At the talk of food, Maggie's stomach growled. "I guess my stomach is saying yes."

The following morning flew by as they handled their bank loan and put the money into the checking account. The next stop was the courthouse. They decided to stop by the sheriff's office first to find out if they had picked Gary up, but no one was in to talk with them. They headed over to the treasurer's office. The woman behind the counter looked familiar, and when it was their turn, the woman looked shocked to see them standing there.

"Wait a minute. You're Jessie's mom, right? I knew I recognized you. I'm Maggie Chesney, and this is Robert."

"Oh my. Yes. Yes. I'm Jessie's mom. What can I do for you two today?"

"Mrs. Keller, we're here to clear up the back taxes."

"Really? All of them? Oh my. Oh my. Let me see what to do about that." Mrs. Keller went to the filing cabinet and continually talked to herself and flipped through files. The other office girl occasionally looked over at her as she helped other customers and shook her head. "I need to make a phone call. I'll be right back." With that, Mrs. Keller rushed out of the office and left Robert and Maggie looking at each other.

"What shall we do now?"

"If she doesn't get back pretty soon, we'll have someone else wait on us."

Maggie shrugged, and they stood there and waited until the other customers had completed their business. Robert walked over and asked the other office person to help them, and after approximately fifteen minutes, the taxes and penalties were paid, and a receipt was in hand. They never did see Mrs. Keller again as they left the courthouse.

"That was really weird. What got into her anyway?"

"I have no idea, but you were going to call Luke when we were done."

"All this took longer than I planned. How about we meet him for lunch?"

"Sounds like a good idea. I'd like to actually meet the guy who has sparked an interest in my sister's life."

"Stop it. We're just friends."

"Uh huh."

She called Luke, and he met them at the Chinese restaurant a few minutes later. Robert and Luke spent most of lunch getting to know each other, and they both practically ignored Maggie. She finally cleared her throat loudly to get their attention. "Excuse me, but I have a dog to go check on if anyone cares enough to let me get there." The men jumped up and argued over who was paying the bill before they finally got out the door.

"Luke, go on ahead and take her to the vet's office. I'll make a couple of phone calls to work and stop by the sheriff's office to follow up on what is going on. I'll meet you back at the house."

Maggie rushed in to see King. "Hank! How's my dog?"

"Come this way and see." Hank led them through the office to a quiet room in the back. King was lying in a large kennel, still swaddled in gauze. "The bleeding stopped last night, and so far, he hasn't had any further problems."

Maggie sat down in front of King and put her hand out for King to smell. Slowly, his tongue came out and gave her hand a small lick. She leaned over and hugged the dog carefully and talked to him while petting his head. Luke and Hank walked out and visited between customers. After an hour, Luke managed to get Maggie to leave King for the day.

"You can come back anytime tomorrow. Let's get you home. You've had a tough couple of days."

Luke dropped Maggie off at home and made sure Robert was there before leaving. Robert sat Maggie down at the kitchen table and asked her to talk about her dog. Maggie explained how the dog knew she was there, so she felt better about King getting better, but it was going to take a while. Robert listened but was fidgeting with the salt and black pepper shakers.

"What's the matter with you? You're antsy!"

"Gary Johnson slipped away from the sheriff's office. They have an all-points bulletin out on him. How he managed, I don't know, but they want us to be careful."

"Robert, those files didn't have anything worth taking. Once he looks through everything he's going to come back. I don't know what he wants or where else to look. I don't want this house torn up again. It isn't fair! I'm a nervous wreck as it is!"

"We need to find whatever it is first. Starting tomorrow, we'll keep looking. I've looked around the house, but you did a good job cleaning, so I don't think it's in here. We'll start with the shed. Which reminds me, I brought that trunk in and set it on the back porch. I hate to break that latch. Maybe Luke can open it without breaking it. Speaking of locks, here is the new front door key."

Maggie took the key and tucked it in her pocket. "I'll get it on the key chain later. That trunk should have a key here somewhere. I keep forgetting to look for it."

"Well, I'm not going to worry over it tonight. Maybe it will have the answers we are looking for."

"Or it will be filled with junk like everything else I've gone through."

CHAPTER 9

The next few days went by slowly as Robert and Maggie spent the mornings going through the outbuildings. During the hot part of the day, Robert spent his afternoons making calls and working on his laptop, and Maggie drove over to see King. He was recovering and was always glad to see Maggie arrive. Hank thought that she could take him home the following week as long as no signs of infection had set in. Maggie was able to take him on a short walk in the building, but King wasn't strong enough to go outside.

No one had heard or seen anything out of Gary Johnson. The sheriff's office thought he may have left the area, but no one knew. They asked the Chesneys to remain alert but to go on with their lives. The deputies patrolled their area more often, and she could see a spotlight scanning the yard during the night as they drove by. Robert chose to leave the .410 by the front door just in case he needed it.

Toward the end of the second week, Maggie was able to bring King home. She brought him into the house during the hot part of the day and let him stay outside at night. He was able to wander the yard without difficulty, but she found him resting often in various areas of the yard, as if he would get tired and just lay down where he was. Hank told her he would heal up in time, and King would only do what he could for the time being. It was the way with animals.

Luke was catching up on some repair work and was able to come to the farm occasionally for supper. Robert and Luke had become fast friends, and they all enjoyed sitting on the new deck or under Maggie's favorite elm. Maggie had a list of repairs for Luke to handle when he was caught up and had spare time. At the top of the list was to open the trunk lock.

Now that King was home, Robert was getting ready to leave. They had gone through everything in the outbuildings and had found no files or money. They organized each building and had contacted an auctioneer about selling the antiques and tools.

"I have to get back to work, and I miss my family. The kids are ready to go back to school, so I need to go home. I can come back in a few weeks after things are settled at home. I contacted Dad's lawyer, and he'll start the process of settling the estate. We have the bills caught up, and things should clear pretty quickly. "

"It has been wonderful having you here. And thanks for going through your room and getting rid of stuff. I knew you'd want to keep a few things."

Robert laughed. "Well, I'm surprised at the stuff I found under my bed. Gross!"

"I know I need to let you get packed for your trip, but the one thing I forgot to have you look at was the little chest that held Mom's things. It's still sitting in the corner of the kitchen out of the way."

They went over to the chest and brought it to the living room where they had more room. Since Robert was a little older when she died, he could remember his mother. They started with the first drawer and looked at her jewelry. "You know, all the stuff in the bedroom was messy except this chest. Dad must have loved Mother very much to have kept her things so neat and tidy. He probably looked at these things a million times over the years. There wasn't even a lot of dust on top now that I think about it."

Robert fingered through the jewelry and picked up the wedding band. "I remember I got scratched by the setting on this one time when I was little. She was trying to get me to settle down, and I jerked from her. I had a long scratch on my arm from it, and I thought she did it on purpose at the time because I was being so naughty." He returned it to its place. "I think you're right, though. Dad loved her very much."

They pulled open the second drawer, and Maggie pushed aside the scarves. The mementos were from their parents honeymoon in Hawaii. It was an extravagant thing to do at the time, but they both remembered their dad talking about how that was the only trip they ever made, and it was a memory he always cherished.

The third drawer were the love letters, and neither one wanted to read them. Maggie fingered the ribbons. "I think we should just leave them alone. Since we were able to keep the place, I should probably put the chest back into the bedroom where it was."

"Good plan. What's in the bottom drawer?"

"I don't know. I never got past the love letters before I quit looking."

Robert chuckled and pulled on the bottom drawer. It was stuck, and he tugged a little harder. The chest almost tumbled over. "Maybe it isn't a real drawer."

They took the chest out to the kitchen table and held it so part of it was hanging over while Maggie looked under it. "No, there's a drawer there. I don't know why it won't open. Maybe there's something stuck in it." Maggie banged a little bit on the bottom of the drawer, and she could hear something jangle. She looked up at Robert. "There is definitely something in there. Shall we take everything out of the other drawers so we can turn this on its side?"

"Let's try one more time. I hate to disturb the contents." Robert moved the chest to stabilize it, and Maggie tried one more time to pull the drawer. She tugged a few times, and it started to give.

"You pull on it. It might be ready to come out now." Maggie held onto the chest, and Robert gave the drawer a couple more jerks. The drawer finally gave way, and Robert and the drawer both fell backward. Once they recovered from the shock of the fall, they looked down at the drawer's contents.

*   *   *   *   *

Gary Johnson had driven as fast as he could to hit the interstate. He drove to the next exit and took some back roads to catch Highway 30 several miles down. He kept going until he got to the Wyoming border and pulled into a motel off the beaten path with advertising to entice hunters to stay. He went in to register and used yet another fake ID and asked if he could get a room toward the back. He paid cash for a couple of weeks and drove his car in front of his room. He unlocked the door and realized he had plenty of space to work, so he spent the next several minutes hauling boxes of files into the room. Gary took a deep breath and brought in the few personal items he had managed to gather together before taking off. Before looking through the files, he needed something to eat. The motel owner had pointed out a small café and an attached grocery store a short distance away. He didn't even need to drive. *Good set up, I'd say.* Gary grinned and whistled as he walked down to the café.

The bank examiner had come and gone, and Mr. Jensen was now out of a job. His vice president was promoted to president, and the board decided to monitor the bank's business quite a bit closer. The examiners found that in several instances that Mr. Jensen chose who he lent money to over the vote of the board, and nine times out of ten the women were denied loans, or the applications were never brought before the board. Nothing could prove he had anything to do with Gary Johnson, and all of the banks money was intact. The board fired him for unfair practices and would be spending the next several months repairing the damage that Mr. Jensen had caused over the years. Mr. Canon had even mentioned they might have to look at selling the independent bank because of the loss in business Mr. Jensen had caused.

The realtors' association couldn't find a record of any licensure for Gary Johnson. The sheriff's office ran his prints and found there was a federal warrant out for his arrest for running the same type of scams he was attempting to work in Paxton. Samuel Reitz aka Gary Johnson was wanted in four different states and was known to use a gun in some of his escapades. No one knew exactly why he stole the Chesneys' files, but the sheriff's office didn't believe he was done harassing them. They continued to drive by the farm frequently and monitored local motels and bars for his car.

The sheriff brought Mr. Jensen in for questioning about Gary Johnson, but he claimed he was only his banker and didn't know anything about what he was doing in town. Although no one believed him, there was no evidence to hold him. The sheriff told Mr. Jensen that they would be monitoring his whereabouts and he was not to leave town. After much discussion with the Chesneys and other area residents, the sheriff knew that there was more to the story than anyone was saying, but until they caught up with Gary Johnson, they might never be able to put everything together.

*   *   *   *   *

Robert and Maggie looked at the drawer. It had been purposely glued shut, and part of the frame had come off with the drawer. Maggie reached down and picked up a ring of keys. "Well, well, well. What have we here?"

Robert picked himself up off the floor and put the drawer on the table. "Looks like there is a paper in the drawer too." Robert carefully lifted a small folded paper off the bottom of the drawer and opened it up carefully. The writing was his father's, and it was addressed to them both.

To My Children:

I have no idea how long it took for you to open the drawer and find this note, but I hope this finds you both well. Your mother and I loved you very much, and I hope you will always be as happy as we were in the short time we were allowed to be together.

I don't really know what is happening to me, but I'm forgetting things more and more. I don't know if I'm paranoid or if there is a reason to not trust a lot of people these days. I hope I join your mother soon as I continue to miss her so much, and my life has felt empty since she died.

The keys are a token of my love for you. There should be three of them on the ring. One is the spare to my beloved truck. I hope you take care of her for me. The second one is to the trunk located in front of my pickup in the shed. It holds some information you will need to go forward. The third one is for you to find what it belongs to. Life has its ups and downs. Sometimes things squeak, and sometimes they break. Tread lightly, and don't get too down about things. You can repair just about anything in life. One step at a time, children. One step at a time.

Love, Dad

The two stood there and looked at each other and then the keys. Finally, Maggie broke the silence. "I finally get to see what's in that stupid trunk. Luke has been so busy catching up repairs elsewhere he hasn't had a chance to work on that lock." They went to the back porch and knelt in front of the trunk. Robert checked the lock and chose the key. As he put the key in the lock and was ready to turn it, he looked at Maggie.

"You ready to be disappointed, sis?"

Maggie laughed. "You bet. Let's get this over with and try to figure out what he meant about the third key."

Robert had to twist and turn the lock a few times to get it to open. It finally clicked, and Robert slowly opened the lid. Maggie and Robert both looked at the contents and sat back on their heels.

* * * * *

Gary finished his meal at the Get Lost Café. He chuckled when he saw the name. *How apropos.* He stopped in the attached grocery store and bought some donuts for breakfast and a bottle of juice and wandered back to his room. He was anxious to start looking through the files to retrieve the paperwork he desired. Gary spent the next three hours looking at every shred of paper he had taken and realized there was nothing there. The longer he looked, the angrier he became. He threw the last box across the room and went to stand by the window and stared out into the dark. *Now what am I going to do?*

* * * * *

Maggie finally reached in and pulled out the first of many files. The first one was the deed to the farm, and the following files had the history of purchases their ancestors had made to build it to the current size. As they looked at more files, it included the income tax filings for the last ten years. Maggie looked at the first one and gasped at the amount of money her father said he made. She showed it to Robert. "What the heck? Let's take this trunk up to the living room so we can lay everything out." They each grabbed an end and hauled it to the living room and placed it by the coffee table. Robert took the land files and placed them in a pile as Maggie took the income tax files and laid them beside her. As they continued to look at the last remaining files, Maggie noticed one with the title "Taxes." As she pulled out the folder, some receipts fell out. She picked the papers up and opened up the folder. Each one of them was a receipt from the courthouse when her father paid the taxes . . . in cash.

"Robert." Maggie pulled on his arm to show him the file. "Robert. Look at this."

Robert took the file and leafed through the receipts for the last ten years. "Are you kidding me? Cash?"

"You know what this means, don't you?"

Finally, Maggie and Robert knew why Mrs. Keller was so nervous. Their father had paid cash for the taxes, but it had never been registered paid. "All she did was fill out a receipt for payment and evidently took the money for herself."

"I think we need to call our best friends at the sheriff's office. Maybe we found some connection to Gary Johnson after all."

The sheriff himself arrived shortly after being called. He looked at the files, and after discussing what happened with Mrs. Keller when they had gone to the courthouse to pay the delinquent taxes, the sheriff shook his head. "This case is getting more complicated all the time. I'll have to take the tax files as evidence for now. Maybe after we have a conversation with Mrs. Keller, we will have more answers."

Maggie requested she make a quick copy of the receipts, and the sheriff agreed. As Maggie hurriedly scanned them into her computer, the sheriff looked at the rest of the files. When he came to the deed, he paused. "Wait a minute. Let me look at that deed again." Robert handed him the current deed, and the sheriff looked it over. Maggie finished what she was doing and brought the file back to the sheriff. "Look at the deed. See where your father signed this?" They both looked at it and nodded. "The way he left it signed was probably for you two to decide if you wanted both your names on it or just one of you. As it is, anyone can sign their name to this deed and own it free and clear."

Everyone looked at each other and, at the same time, said, "Gary Johnson."

Robert asked the question they all wondered. "How would he know that the deed wasn't filled out yet?"

The sheriff scratched his head. "I don't know, but if I were you, I'd get this put in a safe place. Like a bank deposit box. I could take it as evidence for a while, but I don't think I've got enough proof that Gary was looking for this specifically."

Robert and Maggie agreed to take it to the bank on their way to North Platte tomorrow to drop Robert off to catch his plane, but Maggie made a copy of the signature page, wrote on it COPY, and gave it to the sheriff just in case it was needed.

The sheriff left for the office, and Maggie and Robert decided to put the files back in the trunk and carried it to their father's closet. There wasn't anything they needed out of it except the deed, and Maggie had already put that in her purse after both of them signed it. The sheriff signed his name as a witness below it as a precaution.

The sheriff radioed ahead and had a deputy go to Mrs. Keller's place to bring her to the office for questioning. He was on his way back and would be there about the same time he figured it would take for them to get her and bring her down. Mrs. Keller panicked at the sight of a deputy on her doorstep and fainted. Mr. Keller came running at the noise of her falling and sat fretting over his wife. The deputy squatted down and looked at Mrs. Keller's pale features and decided he needed to call an ambulance. The sheriff heard the call go out and headed to the hospital instead. The deputy informed him of what had happened at the house.

After Mrs. Keller was looked after, the doctor came out and asked what was going on. "I'm not at liberty to say, exactly, but we were going to question her about embezzlement of funds." The doctor scratched his chin.

"Her labs and EKG didn't show a heart attack, so I'm thinking she probably just fainted and hit her head. The CAT scan didn't show any damage, either."

"Will you be keeping her then?"

"I should. We usually monitor patients throughout the night in case something shows up later."

"Can I talk to her now, or do I need to wait until morning?"

Mr. Keller walked over to the men. "Sheriff, you can get a statement now. My wife is going to be in a terrible state all night if you wait. We both decided you need to take a statement now."

The doctor looked at the sheriff. "You have your answer, but I still want to keep her overnight."

"That's fine. We'll see what she has to say."

The sheriff and his deputy walked into the ER with Mr. Keller. They asked the nurse to leave for a while and would notify her when they were done. The nurse looked over at the doctor, and he nodded his head. They left the room, closing the door behind them.

"Mrs. Keller, I'm Sheriff Campbell, and I believe you have met my deputy here. He will be taking your statement on tape, and then I will need you to come to the office tomorrow after your release and sign a written statement. Do you want me to ask questions, or do you just want to start from the beginning?"

"I'll just start."

The sheriff nodded at his deputy. "Okay. First of all, in the room are Sheriff Campbell, Deputy Pierce, and Mr. and Mrs. Keller. It is 10:00 p.m., and we are in the Ogallala Hospital ER, and the staff is not in the room at this time. Mr. and Mrs. Keller have agreed to a recording of their statement at this time and to come to the office to sign a transcript of this statement. Do you agree to this? If so, both of you say yes." Both of the Keller's agreed, and Mrs. Keller took a deep breath.

* * * * * * *

Gary Johnson woke up late the next morning with a terrible headache. He had gone to the bar after wasting his time on the files and tried to drown his sorrows. It didn't work, and he felt worse today. Gary looked around the mess he had made of the room and groaned. The maid would have a fit. He got up and made sure the privacy lock was on and took a hot shower. Once he ate a couple of donuts, took a couple of aspirin, and drank his juice, he almost felt human again. He went out and turned his car around so the trunk was facing the door and popped it open. Gary grabbed file after file and threw them in the trunk and then took the boxes out to the dumpster. He had just finished when the maid came around the corner. She asked if she could get him some clean towels and sheets, and he nodded to go on ahead. He stood out by his car and tried to will his headache to go away completely. The maid finished her work quickly, and Gary went back into the room. He left the door open as he wasn't sure if he was staying or going. He hadn't come up with any answers yet and was becoming more frustrated by the minute. Gary tried to figure out how to find what he was looking for without getting caught. It was just a matter of time.

* * * *

Mrs. Keller began by discussing her husband's illness a few years ago. It had taken him out of the workforce, and between the medical bills and their living expenses, she didn't make enough money to pay the bills.

"When Mr. Chesney came into the treasurer's office one day, I realized I could take his cash, and no one would be the wiser. I thought that I could eventually catch up paying for everything or get a loan and pay it back. I went to see Mr. Jensen at the bank, and he laughed me out of the bank. He said if I wanted money, I would have to send my husband in to see him. I couldn't let my husband know I took the money, so there was no way I could explain why we needed to borrow so much. Then Mr. Chesney came back six months later to pay more taxes with cash, and I just kept taking it. My daughter Jessie sells real estate, and she was having a hard time in this economy, and I would give her money now and then to help her out. Mr. Chesney just kept coming in every six months and paid cash, and I always waited on him. I think he started to catch on before he died, but he never said anything to anyone. I knew I was running out of time because the delinquent notice was going to go out again. I had intercepted his mail previously, so I tried to keep him from knowing."

"That's when Gary Johnson showed up one day. He said he was opening an office in town and wanted to buy all the property with the back taxes on it. I was relieved because the money would be paid back to the county, but I didn't know how I was going to explain it away to Mr. Chesney. The web of deceit just got bigger and bigger. When Mr. Chesney died, I was relieved. I knew he would never find out, and I was finally in the clear. Then his kids came in to pay the back taxes, and I couldn't look them in the eye. I fell apart, went home, and called in sick. I had to tell my husband what I had done."

Mr. Keller sat there holding his wife's hand, an occasional tear rolling down his face. "I didn't realize she took that money, and if I had, I would have made sure it got paid back somehow."

"Mrs. Keller, you heard about us trying to arrest Gary Johnson."

"Yes."

"Why do you think he was at the Cheney's place taking files?"

"I don't know. He always talked big plans. He would go to my daughter's office and brag about buying places for back taxes and selling them for a profit. Jessie talked to me about trying to do that if she could come up with some money. I discouraged her because I saw what it was doing to an elderly couple he kicked out of their home."

"After the Chesneys paid the back taxes, did you pay Gary Johnson back?"

"I had to. I wasn't going to screw anyone else out of their money. Why?"

"Did he cash his check or deposit it? Do you know?"

"I have no idea. He and Mr. Jensen were thick as thieves. You always saw them together for meals at Ole's. I haven't talked to Gary for a couple of weeks."

"Do you have anything else you want to tell us?"

"I'm sorry for what I've done. I'll be down tomorrow to sign my statement and go from there."

"Mr. Keller? You have anything else?"

Mr. Keller shook his head. "No."

"We have completed the statement of Mr. and Mrs. Keller at 11:03 p.m."

Mrs. Keller looked up at the sheriff, her face wan and etched with fear and anxiety. "Are you going to arrest me?"

"I'll do that when you come to the office. Right now you both need to rest, and I trust you will show up as soon as you are discharged from here. Don't let me down."

"I won't, Sheriff. Thank you. I feel better now that I've told you about everything."

*　*　*　*　*

Robert and Maggie opened a safety deposit box and placed the deed inside. Maggie decided to put her mother's wedding rings in the box too. She hadn't found anything else of enough value to tuck away. They headed to the airport in North Platte, and Maggie saw Robert safely away. They never had a chance to figure out what their father meant about the third key, but they knew it would keep for another day.

Maggie returned home and walked into a quiet house. She decided to get the mail and then check her e-mail. As she waited for her computer to boot up, she walked out to the mailbox with King walking beside her. He was doing much better and was even chasing after rabbits. When Maggie got back to the house, her e-mail was waiting. As she looked through her inbox, she found one from the school system and clicked on it excitedly. They were anxious to meet her and requested she call for a meeting. Maggie smiled and knew she was ready to get back to a routine again. She needed to move out of her apartment and haul her belongings to the farm before she accepted any assignments. She called her landlord and set a date by the end of September. She felt that would give her plenty of time to pack up her apartment and get everything home.

Luke was able to come by occasionally and do some repair work. Maggie wanted the outbuildings repaired before fall weather set in, and then she could concentrate on some home repairs. Luke had a list and could come and go when he was available, and Maggie didn't need to be home since he was working outside. They would occasionally go out for a meal, or Maggie would cook something at the house. They were becoming fast friends and enjoyed each other's company. King would follow Luke around and watch him work.

Maggie had been talking to the auctioneer, and they were planning to set up an auction that fall. He thought there were enough items to have their own sale. The auctioneer's team would pull everything outside of the buildings and use the yard for household items. Once Maggie closed her apartment and brought her own things for the house, she would be able to auction off some of her own personal items along with stuff from the house. She had a plan for the future, and life had finally settled down.

Little did she realize that occasionally Gary Johnson would drive by at different times of the day to see if she was home. He wanted to stop in and check the house again but couldn't do it if he would be seen. He was becoming more anxious as the days flew by. Gary thought it necessary to move from his motel as to not cause suspicion. He drove south for thirty miles until he found another off-the-beaten path motel to use for a while. Gary was driving by slowly and didn't see any car in the driveway. He pulled behind the row of cedars, slowly got out, and peered through the trees to monitor for activity. Not seeing anyone, he continued toward the shed where he knew Maggie kept her car. He quietly walked up and saw that the car was gone.

Gary strode up to the house and worked on jimmying the back-door lock. It took almost ten minutes, and he had to use a screw-driver to split the wood before it would open. He walked in and listened for any sounds; then he walked through the kitchen and into the living room. Everything looked the same as when he was there previously. He hurried through to the den and checked the file drawers and noted they were still empty. He opened the bedroom door, and every drawer was empty except the chest in the corner. He opened each one, but it held nothing he was looking for. Gary slid the closet open and saw the trunk. He popped the lid open and saw files. Gary grinned and gathered them up in his arms and headed for the door, but just as he was leaving, he heard a truck come into the yard. He poked his head around the door and looked out. The truck drove on to an outbuilding and stopped. He decided he was going to leave and stay on the back side of the house when he saw the dog. *I thought I killed that critter!* Gary stopped and waited until he saw the dog follow the man in the truck to one of the buildings. He slid out the door and took off for the cedar trees, trying to stay out of sight or smell of the dog. Just as he got into the car and backed out, he could hear the dog barking and saw it headed his way. Gary headed down the road and left the dog in his dust.

Luke watched King as he took off running, barking and growl-ing. He thought he better follow and tried to keep up. He was more worried about King stressing himself than what he was barking at. When Luke saw the car take off for the road, he called the sheriff's office and told them he thought Gary Johnson had come back and what direction he was headed. Luke walked back to the house as he talked to the dispatcher and saw the back door open. He reported the break in also. A deputy was on the way to the house, and a notification to all area law enforcement agencies went out about Gary being seen again.

Luke stood there and waited for King to come back. King had chased the car a half a mile before giving up, and as he came back, he began walking slower the closer he got to the house. Luke sat down and held him while waiting for the deputy to show up and made sure King had plenty of water. Luke checked his old injury to make sure it hadn't reopened, but everything looked fine, and King seemed to be recovering. As the deputy drove into the yard, King jumped up and started to growl. Luke calmed him and told King to sit. The deputy came over, and Luke explained what he had seen and showed him the back-door lock and doorjamb.

Ten minutes later, Maggie pulled in and immediately knew Gary Johnson had returned. She grabbed the groceries that needed to be put in the refrigerator and got out of the car. "What did he do now?"

"Broke into the house, but he got away before King could catch him."

"Poor King. He looks exhausted."

"He chased Gary down the road for a ways, but I gave him water and have been making him stay right here."

Maggie reached down and petted King. "Come on, boy. Let's go into the house for bit where it's cooler." King followed Maggie and lay in the living room while she put her groceries away. The deputy followed and waited for Maggie to check the house. The deputy gave her gloves to wear as she checked rooms and drawers. The bedroom closet was open, and so was the chest. Maggie walked over and saw the chest was now empty. "He took all the files from this chest." Maggie sat down on the edge of the bed. "It held some historical documents on the farm and other miscellaneous papers. The sheriff took the file on the tax payments, and we put the deed in the safety deposit box. If it hadn't been for the sheriff noticing the deed being signed but not designated to anyone, he would have had it too. He'll be back. I'm pretty sure that is what he was after now."

Luke had walked in and watched Maggie explain the loss to the deputy. He walked over and sat beside her and took her hand. "I'll call Robert for you. Will you be all right?"

Maggie looked at Luke and then at their hands folded together. "Thanks for being here, Luke. It means a lot to me. Thanks for offering to call Robert. I'm too upset to call him right now. My phone is on the counter."

Gary hightailed it back to the motel and quickly pulled up to his room and got out. He bundled the files together after getting his room key out, and once in the room, he threw them on the bed. Gary tore through each one of them, looking for the deed. He found all the old information on the farm, but the deed was gone. "She found it. I knew it! I waited too long! If that old man hadn't hid it from me to begin with, I'd have possession of the place by now!" Gary smacked the stack of files, and they flew all over the room. He grabbed a pillow and screamed into it until he felt a little better. "Crap!" Gary looked around at the mess he made. He once again had a mess to clean up. Gary grabbed a trash bag and threw the papers in it. Once he had it all picked up, he took it to his car and threw it in the trunk with everything else. He went back to his room and packed his stuff. "Time to move again." Gary hit the road in search of another motel.

Law enforcement in three states was currently looking for Gary. He didn't know it, but they were close. The Wyoming sheriff's deputy stopped at every motel he could think of that was in out-of-the-way places. In the first motel Gary had stayed, the owner remembered Gary being there and was glad when he had moved on. He told the officer that Gary "*creeped* him out." The sheriff's office expanded their search and began looking at several motels similar to the first. As a deputy pulled up to the second motel, he had missed Gary by two hours. The search was on.

CHAPTER 10

Luke picked Maggie up for church on Sunday, and she asked to be put on the prayer list for her safety and the capture of Gary Johnson. The sheriff's office had stepped up their concentrations in the area of the farm, and Luke had trimmed back the cedar trees so Gary couldn't hide the car from the road. It seemed as that was his favorite hiding spot, and no one wanted to make it easy for him to sneak up on Maggie. She never went anywhere outside without King by her side. He was back to normal and was very protective of her. King stayed close by her side as she strolled out to get the mail, worked in the yard, or walked to the pond. Robert called Maggie daily to check on her, and she was becoming agitated by all the attention. She knew that until Gary was caught, she wasn't safe, but she had a life to lead, and Maggie wasn't going to let fear dictate what she did every day.

Mrs. Keller resigned her position at the courthouse immediately and was charged with embezzlement. Maggie and Robert asked for restitution only. They felt she was going to have to live with her decision no matter what the courts decided. They also knew that the Keller's would probably never be able to pay them back as the amount of money was extensive, and neither one was holding down a job at this time.

Maggie set up an interview for a temp teaching position on Wednesday and decided to make a day of it getting groceries and some other much-needed stops. In the meantime, she had grass to mow and watering to do.

Luke had finished up the repairs to the outbuildings and was ready to start on the small repairs needed to the inside of the house. He had already fixed the back door and put a plate on the frame so no one could break into the house. Maggie wanted every room painted, and there were a few things such as a broken stair tread and loose handrail. The trim was in good shape, but some of it was starting to come down. The repairs wouldn't take much time, but the painting would require several hours. Maggie was going to help, and Luke was anxious to spend the time with her. He had cleared his own calendar for a week in order to get the painting done all at one time. His father's crew was coming back to paint the outside of the house that fall along with shingling the roof.

Gary had spent the next week changing motel rooms and was going farther and farther away from the farm. He still hadn't figured out what he was going to do, but the anger was growing at losing access to the deed. Gary kept thinking back at how he had snookered old man Chesney and how he was going to make millions once he got a hold of the deed. Gary had pretended to be from the insurance company, and it made it pretty easy to have a look at Mr. Chesney's insurance policy and deed. The old man was becoming addled and didn't have any idea what was going on. Gary made him sign the deed and then told him to put it away. Gary watched as the old man filed it and knew this con was going well. As he thought back on how little time it took to set up the deal, it angered him all the more to find the deed gone. Gary was going to make someone pay.

Maggie went to her interview at the school and was thrilled when they hired her on the spot. They agreed to wait until October before she would be available, and she made arrangements to come back to town another day to the human resource department to sign all her papers and be provided a tour of the schools she would be working with. She felt lighthearted as she shopped for paint and accessories, then stopped at the grocery store on the way home. Luke was coming over for supper that evening, and she wanted to fix him something special to celebrate her new job.

Maggie and Luke enjoyed the pot roast supper and went outside on the deck to enjoy the evening. Luke grabbed the ice tea, and Maggie brought the apple pie and ice cream. They watched the evening fold in on them as they talked about the projects for the following week. Maggie told him about the colors she had picked out for each room. She was trying to stay with similar colors so they wouldn't have to prime it first.

"When I cleaned each room, I washed down the walls, so they are ready to paint when you are."

"I'll be here bright and early on Monday. Another thing, I'd like to help you pack up your apartment when you're ready. Do you mind if I go along?"

"Oh my! That is awfully generous of you. Let me think." Maggie paused for a little bit, mulling it over. "I think what would be better is that I go on down and go through things, pack up, and then you could come down and help me load the U-Haul. I plan on getting a car trailer so you could drive the truck back if you wanted to."

"I like the sound of that. That will give you personal time to say good-bye to friends too. Just let me know when you plan on going so I can clear my calendar."

"Let's plan on a Saturday so you won't miss any work. I want to make sure that I have the house painted and repaired ahead of time, and once we get that done, I'll make the reservation for my U-Haul. Some of this stuff we'll have to move for the painting, so I'm thinking we'll take it out to the shop for now, and it will be ready for the auction. It will be out of the house, and I can throw an old sheet over things like the couch to keep the dirt off."

"I'm game. I'll bring a furniture mover, and I'll call one of my brothers to help. Some of that furniture will be mighty heavy since it was made a long time ago and when it was actually made to last."

Maggie laughed. "You're right. My furniture is nothing in weight in comparison to the old couches I was moving around in there."

They visited until well after dark. Luke finally got up to leave. "Thanks for supper. I've enjoyed the company." Luke reached over and took Maggie's hands and helped her stand up. He held her close and tipped his head down to kiss her lightly on the lips. He smiled, and Maggie smiled back. Luke continued to hold her close. "Maggie, I like where this is going."

Maggie looked up shyly and smiled. "Me too."

Luke kissed her quickly and let her go. "I'll talk to you later." Luke jumped in the truck and waved as he drove out of the yard. Maggie reached up and touched her tingling lips. *Me too.*

Gary woke up with another hangover. He had been drinking heavily since he was on the run. Maggie didn't know he had still been driving by occasionally, and Gary was always missed by law officers attempting to locate him. The changing of motels so frequently kept them at bay. Gary decided to move to someplace closer to the farm and found a motel in a town twenty minutes away. He had been seeing a lot of police presence in Colorado and Wyoming and decided to move back into Nebraska. Gary chuckled as he thought about how he was leading them on a merry chase. He settled into the new motel and decided he needed fresh clothes since he had been wearing the same ones over and over. Gary waited until just before dark and went to his old apartment, walked in, and retrieved several changes of clothes and other personal items. He laughed as he drove away, knowing he had snookered the cops once again.

The following week, Luke brought his brother Mark over, and they moved the old couches and other furniture out to the shop for storage until the auction. Mark offered to help paint that week, as his schedule was pretty light. Maggie appreciated the extra help and made sure that Mark was paid well for his efforts. By the end of the week, the whole inside of the house had a new coat of paint on it and looked much brighter and cleaner. They celebrated by going to the steak house in North Platte on Saturday night. The three of them had a good time that week and spent the evening laughing over spilled paint and other antics the two brothers committed.

It was mid-September, and Maggie made plans to close out her apartment now that the painting was done. She scheduled a U-Haul pickup later in the week and planned to leave on Tuesday to work on emptying the apartment. She planned to bring everything she had with her and then decide if she wanted to put some of her own things on the auction. By Monday afternoon, she was packed and ready to go. She didn't need to bring any clothes with her as she had a closet full at the apartment. Maggie decided to walk down to the pond and brought a chair with her. She sat down and watched the late-fall wildflowers and grass blowing in the breeze and the frogs catching bugs. This was always a peaceful time for her, and King lay beside her quietly. The pond had continued to be recharged all summer by occasional rains, and the grass surrounding it was lush. She always kept an area mowed for her path to and from the pond and for her to sit and enjoy her time because she wasn't too interested in walking or sitting on a snake hiding in the grass.

King started a low growl and sat up and sniffed the air. He continued to growl and look around. Maggie reached over to him. "What do you smell, boy?" Maggie felt the hair on the back of her neck stand up. King stood on all fours and began barking in earnest and looking behind her. Maggie slowly stood up and turned. There, before her, was Gary Johnson holding a gun on them both.

Maggie kept a hand on her dog and quietly told King to sit. "What do you want?"

Gary waved the gun toward King. "I want you to make sure that mongrel doesn't attack me, or I'll make sure I kill him this time."

"No, I mean what do you want from me?"

Gary gave her a wicked grin and then looked around. He waved the gun around and pointed toward the house. "Let's get out of sight. Walk over to the shed first, and lock the dog inside."

Maggie noticed that Gary looked very nervous and kept looking around. She didn't want him to shoot King again, and King was shaking. Maggie talked softly to the dog and urged him to walk with her to the shed. After coaxing King into the shed and told him to stay, she shut the door. Maggie could hear the dog alternately whimper than bark. "Good dog, King. Stay." Maggie turned from the closed door.

Gary shoved her to get her moving, then grabbed her arm and pulled her toward the house.

"Open the door." Maggie opened the back door and left it wide open. Gary followed and slammed the door closed. "I don't want any attempts at you leaving. Get upstairs."

Maggie did as she was told and walked to the living room. Gary waved her over to the only couch left in the room, and she sat down.

"Now. Why don't you tell me what you've done with the deed? I've looked all over for it."

"Why do you want the deed? You know everyone in the surrounding area is looking for you. You won't be able to do anything with the deed even if you took it. No one will trust you again."

Gary started to yell, "I didn't ask for a running commentary on what you think about anything. I want the deed, and I want it now!"

"I don't have it."

"What do you mean you don't have it? I know it was in the files, and now it's not. Where is it?"

"I don't have it. If you don't have it and I don't have it, then it isn't here."

Gary reached over and slapped her across the face so hard it knocked her over on the couch. Maggie screamed and saw stars. She lay there holding her face and looking up at Gary.

Gary yelled at her again, "I'm not going to ask you again! Where is the deed?"

"I told you. It's not here."

Gary reached over to hit her again, but Maggie threw herself to the floor and scrambled out of his way.

"Just go and leave me alone. I don't have it."

Gary kicked out at Maggie, but she scooted away, and his dress shoe glanced off her shin. She grimaced at the pain. She tried to get up, and Gary reached over and grabbed her by the arm and yanked her off the floor, then slapped her again so hard she fell sideways to the couch and bounced to the floor. He kicked her in the stomach and knocked the air out of her. She lay still in agony and tried to pretend he had knocked her out. Gary reached down and lifted her head by her hair, and Maggie kept her eyes shut and tried to not call out in pain. He dropped her, and her head bounced off the floor, and Maggie passed out.

Gary turned and went to the den and looked in the file drawers and saw they were still empty. He went back to the trunk and saw that nothing had been added since he took the files. He glanced around and decided to look around the house. Gary checked on Maggie and saw she was still lying on the floor passed out, so he continued searching the house. Maggie had awakened quickly but lay there quietly and listened to Gary tear through the house. When he went downstairs to search, Maggie quickly reached into her back pocket to grab her phone and dialed 911. She lifted her head and quietly told the dispatcher to send someone out quickly because she was being attacked. Maggie left the phone connected and placed it on a shelf of the coffee table. She heard Gary coming back up the steps, so she laid her head back down and closed her eyes.

Gary reached down and grabbed Maggie by the arm and dragged her across the room and propped her up against a wall. Maggie whimpered at the pain shooting throughout her body. Gary reached down and slapped her hard again. "If you want the beating to stop, you better tell me where the deed is."

Maggie whispered through swollen lips. "It's not here, or I'd give it to you."

Gary reached over and slapped her again. Maggie screamed at the pain. He kicked her legs, and she howled. "Are you going to tell me now?"

"It's not here."

Gary kicked her in the gut, and she folded over and passed out. *Great. Now I'm going to have to wait until she wakes up again. Then I'll threaten to shoot her.* Gary reached into his back pocket and brought out a flask. He drank the alcohol until it was almost gone. He looked down at Maggie and realized she was still out. Gary decided he better keep looking, so he started to tear through the kitchen cupboards. Maggie lay there in pain, waking up to the noise in the next room. She needed to either wait for the sheriff's department to get there, or she had to figure out how to get to the pantry. The shotgun had been put away while they were painting, and the pantry was the safest place. Maggie didn't know if she could use it or not, but thought if he continued to threaten her, she wanted to be armed. Her body hurt all over, and as she did inventory of her injuries, Maggie figured she probably couldn't lift the heavy barrel up enough to fire it anyway. She gave up on the idea and decided to wait for help as there was no other choice.

Gary quit searching in the kitchen and came back to check on Maggie. He sat her back up and pressed her against the wall. "I have a gun, and I'm not afraid to use it. Are you going to tell me or not?"

He kicked her in the stomach again. Maggie was dizzy, and the light bothered her eyes. The next thing she knew she was throwing up all over Gary's shoes and pants. He jumped back and cussed at her until he was blue in the face. "Are you kidding me? I should shoot you just for puking on me! Aaugh!"

Maggie fell over to the floor, closed her eyes, and wrapped her arms around her stomach. Inside she chuckled at the circumstances, but she was still so dizzy she couldn't sit up. Gary had gone to the kitchen sink and was trying to clean himself up when he heard a click of a gun. He stopped what he was doing and turned around.

"Samuel Rietz, aka Gary Johnson, you are under arrest." Maggie opened one eye and saw Sheriff Campbell and three deputies standing before Gary. Gary dropped the wet towel he had been using to clean himself and held up his arms. As two of the deputies cuffed Gary and led him to a car, Sheriff Campbell radioed for an ambulance then sat down beside Maggie and put her head in his lap. Maggie began to bawl.

"Call Luke for me."

At the hospital, Luke came running into the ER and had to be stopped by the nurses. "Son, we need to take care of her first before we can let you in there." Luke reluctantly sat in the waiting room with Sheriff Campbell while the staff continued to check Maggie over and did a CAT scan and X-rays. Luke called Robert to tell him about his sister, and Robert agreed that even if she was going to be fine, he was going to fly out as soon as he could. When Robert called back, he told Luke he could be there tomorrow and would rent a car at the airport.

Two hours later, the doctor came out and told both the Sheriff and Luke they could go in and see her before taking her to surgery. Luke rushed to Maggie's bedside and gasped at her bruised face and split lips. One eye was so swollen she could hardly see through it.

"Oh, Maggie! I'm so sorry he did this to you!" Maggie reached out to Luke, and he took her hand.

"I'll be fine. Bruised, not broken. Sore." She could hardly talk from the pain in her mouth.

Sheriff Campbell gently patted her on the shoulder. "I can see it's difficult for you to talk. I'll come see you in the morning, and I'll get a statement from you when you are able." Maggie nodded. The sheriff shook Luke's hand and walked out of the ER. The nurses finished preparing her for surgery, and Luke followed the cart holding Maggie's hand. The nurses pointed to the waiting room and took Maggie through the double doors.

Luke paced in the waiting room and down the hallway to get a glass of tea. His emotions were all over the place. First he was livid with Gary Johnson, and then he was afraid for Maggie, scared of the surgery, and frightened of the unknown. Luke was told she had some internal bleeding, and the surgeon was going to explore her abdomen to find it. His attempts at praying for her were invaded by his fears. Just as he was becoming exasperated, a nurse came to the waiting room and told Luke that the surgery was completed and the doctor would be in soon to see him. Luke flopped on the couch and held his head in his hands.

The surgeon arrived and explained that not only did she have a tear on her kidney; Maggie's spleen was ruptured and needed to be repaired. There would be some long-term recovery for her, but he thought she would heal without incident with time. Luke shook the surgeon's hand and then called Robert to report the latest news. It would be an hour or so before she was transferred to the floor, so Luke, at that moment, went to get something to eat. He asked the nurse which room she would be going to and explained he would be back to spend the night in her room and that her brother would arrive the following day.

Luke grabbed some fast food, went home, and took a quick shower and returned to the hospital. He arrived shortly after she was settled in her room. Luke pulled a chair up to her bed and held her hand. "Don't talk, sweetheart. Rest. I'll be here with you."

"King. Locked in shed."

"I'll call Mark to go let him out and make sure he has water. You're safe now. Get some rest."

Maggie watched as Luke called Mark and explained about King being locked up. The call seemed to help Maggie relax, and she closed her eyes. It seemed only minutes when she awakened and saw Luke sitting by the side of the bed asleep in a chair. She glanced at the clock and saw it was early morning. Maggie tried to turn over and suddenly yelled out in pain. Luke jumped up and focused on his surroundings. "What happened? What can I do to help?"

Maggie attempted a smile, but her lips hurt too much. "Water. I hurt everywhere."

Luke pushed the button for the nurse to come in, then reached over to get Maggie's cup of water. She was able to sip a little bit and wet her mouth and then was able to take a few more swallows. Her lips were still very swollen and sore, but she was able to use a straw to drink. The nurse came in and, after checking her patient over, left to get more pain medication for Maggie. When she returned, the nurse also had a fresh glass of ice water. The nurse helped Maggie reposition in bed and straightened the covers. Maggie closed her eyes and was soon dropping off to sleep. Luke settled back into his chair and thought about what Gary had done to his girl. He was so upset he couldn't get back to sleep. Luke turned the TV on and left the sound off. He found the news and read the crawler to catch up on what was going on around the world.

CHAPTER 11

Maggie spent the next several days in the hospital due to a severe concussion and bruising from head to toe from the beating she took from Gary. It would be awhile for the incision to stop throbbing. Robert had arrived late the afternoon following the attack and had stayed during the daylight hours at the hospital every day. Luke would arrive after work to relieve Robert and sit with her for a few hours before heading for home. On the fifth day, a very sore Maggie was able to go home again, and King was excited to see her. Robert and Maggie sat on the back deck, enjoying the fresh air with King by her side.

"I love it out here." Maggie smiled at her brother. Robert smiled back and looked at the bruising and the black eye.

"I'm glad you didn't have any permanent damage to your eye. He really did a number on you."

"My face is just the part you see. I look like this in a lot of places. Even my scalp hurts. But I'm feeling better every day. I also have some really kickin' pain pills I plan on taking tonight when I go to bed. I've been cutting back during the day and just taking some ibuprofen instead."

"Speaking of which, I moved you into Dad's room, and I put myself into my old room. You need a nice big room since you are making the move permanent. I wanted to tell you that everything looks so nice and clean since you painted. Besides, a master suite is for the master of the house, right?"

Maggie laughed and then groaned and held her sides. "Don't make me laugh, bro. It still hurts too much."

"Sorry. You ready to go in and look at it?"

"Sure."

Robert grabbed her overnight bag, helped Maggie up the stairs, and walked her to the bedroom. He had even brought up some of her knickknacks to help decorate the room. "I love it!" she exclaimed. Maggie walked over to the bed and lay back. "I'm going to take a short nap. The trip home wore me out." Robert threw a light blanket on her and pulled the door partway shut on his way out. He spent the next couple of hours working on his laptop before fixing a light meal. Maggie heard him rattling around the kitchen, and when her stomach growled, she decided to get up. After washing her face and looking at her purple face, she shook her head and immediately groaned. *Rule number one. Do not shake your head.*

Maggie joined Robert in the kitchen and visited about his family while they ate. After lunch, Maggie checked her phone and saw the sheriff had called and left a message. She listened to it and called him back. "Sheriff, come out whenever you want. I'm home now. I appreciate you giving me time to heal some before I had to give you my statement."

The sheriff agreed to come out that afternoon and bring someone to record her statement. Robert promised to sit with her as she relived the attack. In the meantime, she asked Robert to help her walk outside and sit on the back deck with King again. "It helps me relax to have him by my side. Maybe I'll do the statement from there."

Luke called Robert before the sheriff arrived and told him that he'd bring pizza for supper. Robert hadn't had much time to visit with Luke since arriving and was happy to catch up with him that evening. He wanted to know Luke's intentions toward his sister, and Maggie had been pretty closed lipped about their relationship. She had repeatedly told her brother that Luke was a good friend, but seeing Luke spend so much time at the hospital told him that Luke thought of Maggie as more than a good friend. He was working on a plan of action to get the two of them together when the sheriff arrived.

The sheriff and a deputy recorded her statement, and then she read the transcript from the call she made to the dispatcher and what was heard since she left the phone open while being attacked. Everything read just as she remembered it happening, and the sheriff told her when they had her statement typed out, they would bring everything to her for signature. In the meantime, Gary Johnson was sitting in jail with no bond, and the other states he was wanted in were working on extradition to stand trial. The sheriff wasn't sure how things were going to play out, but he did know that Gary would probably never see the light of day again.

The sheriff paused. "Maggie, in the trunk of his car was all the files and papers he took from your house. It's all in evidence right now, but I'll get it back to you."

"There isn't much there I really want except the history of purchasing of land by my ancestors. It has sentimental value."

"Eventually, it will be scanned into a file, and you can have the originals back to do what you want with them. We'll be going now. You take care and get better soon."

"Thanks. I'll try. You keep your end of the bargain and keep Gary locked up."

The sheriff tipped his hat as he left.

"All I have left is the trial. I hate reliving this over and over. It was awful." Maggie teared up, and King moved closer to put his head on her lap. She reached down and sat there, petting him until she relaxed once again.

"It won't be long until it's over now. Tomorrow, we're going to brainstorm the note from Dad and try to figure out what the heck he was talking about. And then I need to call for a flight home. Now that I'm sure you will be all right and Gary is locked up, I can trust to leave you home alone. You always were a troublemaker." Maggie stuck her tongue out at Robert, and they both chuckled.

Luke showed up an hour later and brought two large pizzas. They all went to the kitchen, and Robert gave everyone a glass of tea as they settled down at the table. Luke paused and asked if he could say grace. Robert and Maggie both nodded their heads, and they each reached to hold each other's hands. Luke blessed the meal but also thanked God for providing help when Maggie needed it most and that she was recovering without any serious injuries. He asked for quick healing and a quiet understanding. After saying, "Amen," they dug into the pizza and enjoyed visiting with each other. Robert and Luke monopolized most of the conversation, and Maggie found herself daydreaming more than once.

"Maggie?" Robert reached over and touched her arm.

She jerked her head up. "What?"

"You fell asleep. You better go to bed."

Maggie looked around and found the clock. They had been sitting there for three hours. "When did I nod off?"

"About an hour ago. I hated to wake you, but you about fell out of your chair."

"How embarrassing." Maggie got up and told them both good night and headed to her room. She would take a couple of pain pills first before crawling into bed and take her shower in the morning.

Luke and Robert watched her shuffle to her room. When she closed the door, Robert asked Luke to help him clean up, and then they would go sit on the back deck so they wouldn't disturb her. As they settled into the lounge chairs, they relaxed in the fresh evening air. Robert waited for a few minutes before bringing up Luke's relationship with Maggie. "I know you like my sister, but according to her, you are only good friends. What's your take on it?"

Luke pondered the question, rubbed the back of his neck, reached over, and petted King, then finally looked Robert in the eye. "Honestly, right now I think it's one-sided. I was attracted to your sister from day one. When she agreed to attend church with me, I felt a growing connection. I know we have developed a great friendship, and my dad even likes her, which is saying a lot. Your sister is a wonderful person, but this summer has been pretty tough on her. It's been hard for me to hold back and not push for more than friendship because I could see the turmoil she has been going through. I'm hoping that she can put all of that mess behind her and open her eyes to what could develop between us."

Robert appreciated Luke's sensitivity toward Maggie's feelings. "Well, you have my seal of approval if that makes any difference. She needs to get through the trial before going forward, but I know you will be waiting for her. It means a lot to me that someone will be here after I leave. And that brings me to a whole other set of problems. This was the week she was going to get her stuff and had already ordered the U-Haul. I have a suggestion. You feel like taking a road trip? I can grab her apartment keys, and we can bring everything back. She can sort through it once we get here. I know we won't pack it like she would, but she can't do the heavy lifting right now."

"That's a great idea. I was going to spend the rest of the week working on the house, but we can do that instead. I'll call one or two of my brothers to go with us, and we can get it done quicker. You can do her personal things, and the rest of us can do the furniture."

"Hey, that sounds great. How about we head out first thing in the morning? The U-Haul is waiting for us."

"Sure. Let me call my family and see who can come."

By the time the plans were set, Luke had two brothers along for the ride, and everyone was taking off at 6:00 a.m. Robert was going to leave a note for Maggie because he knew she wouldn't be up yet. He was going to be vague and leave it as a surprise. She needed the quiet time to rest and recuperate anyway.

Maggie awakened at ten the following morning and stretched. The muscles were less than compliant, but she was able to get out of bed without much difficulty. She grabbed a long hot shower and wandered out to the kitchen. Robert had left a pot of coffee heating and a bagel off to the side. *Cinnamon raisin. Yum.* She took the wrapping off, toasted it, and then poured a cup of coffee. Maggie decided to go to the back deck and enjoy the fresh air before it became too hot. The weather was quickly turning to fall, but the afternoon heat was going to hold for the next week. She sat looking around and realized her car was gone. *No wonder it's quiet this morning. Robert must be running an errand.* King joined her on the deck, lying there quietly, his ears twitching. Maggie concentrated on the sounds around her, trying to distinguish what King was listening to. She gave up as it bothered her still tender head. *I didn't know concentrating could be so difficult, King.* She reached down and petted his head, finished her breakfast, and went back in the house.

Maggie finally saw Robert's note. *I'll be back either late tonight or first thing in the morning. I have an errand to run before going back home. See you soon. Don't wait up. Get some rest.*

Wonder what he's up to? Maggie dropped the note on the table and decided to take her laptop out to the deck and wade through e-mails and look at the news. *I've got the whole day to rest, and I plan to do just that.*

Maggie took the time to walk to the mailbox and around the yard for exercise. She walked slowly but felt the kinks working their way out of her sore muscles. That afternoon, she took a short nap and later walked down to the pond. Her chair was still there from when Gary showed up. A chill went down her spine as she thought about how he had sneaked up on her. She moved the chair at an angle so she would have her back more to the pond but was still able to view it. After some time, Maggie realized she couldn't enjoy sitting there and returned to the house, bringing her chair with her. It angered her that she was too skittish to sit in one of her favorite spots. *You're not going to get the best of me!*

Maggie fixed herself a light supper and turned in early. She had no intention of trying to stay up for Robert since he might not make it back until the following day. Maggie decided to take only one pain pill that evening as she was getting stronger and had much less pain. The ibuprofen she had taken during the day seemed to be strong enough, and she felt that if she got along well that night, she would quit taking the prescription. Maggie picked up a book she had been reading and settled in for the night. She only managed to read four pages before dropping off to sleep.

Maggie was awakened by a lot of noise. She heard voices and a lot of coming and going. Once she glanced at the clock and realized it was after ten, she got up and dressed. Maggie couldn't believe her eyes when she walked out into the living room filled with boxes and boxes plus her furniture being hauled in the door. "What the heck is going on?"

Robert walked into the house, holding one end of the couch. "Surprise! We closed up your apartment for you." Robert dropped his half of the couch and caught his breath. "Where do you want this heavy thing?"

"Just put it where the old one was." Maggie looked around and saw Luke, two of his brothers, and his father all working on carrying in boxes and furniture. They were lining boxes along the walls of the kitchen and living room, and Robert was attempting to make sure furniture was placed in appropriate rooms. They stripped the bed Maggie was sleeping in and took the old bed down and out of the room and replaced it with her own. The boys even made her bed back up. Maggie sat and watched them work.

The next thing she knew, the Johanssen women were bringing lunch for everyone and placing it on the kitchen counter and table. Maggie was escorted into the kitchen, and a plate was filled for her, and then she was taken to the back deck to get her out of the way from the traffic. She sat in awe at the activities around her. Then all of a sudden, it stopped. The U-Haul was empty, and the men were getting their meals. Robert and Luke joined her on the deck. The other men sat under the elm tree, and the women sat at the kitchen table. The next thing she knew, the women were on their way home, and the men jumped in their truck and left.

"That was exhausting just watching all of that! I don't know what to say except thank you so much for bringing my things to me!"

Robert reached over to give her a hug. "It's the least I could do for what you've gone through all summer. I turned the keys into the apartment manager and told him to send you your deposit back, but to send me the bill for the cleaning. We weren't the cleanest packing crew on the planet."

"I'm still in awe. It will be nice to have my own things again and see how it all works in the house."

Luke reached over and patted her shoulder. "Robert and I will rearrange the furniture to your liking and move the boxes wherever you need them. We didn't label anything, but we tried to keep the boxes somewhat organized."

"Thanks, Luke. I appreciate everything you have done for me." Maggie looked at Luke and smiled. "And thanks for spending so much time with me in the hospital. I don't know why you did, but I truly did notice."

Luke patted her shoulder again. "My pleasure. What are friends for if you can't count on them to be there in your time of need?"

Maggie chuckled and looked over at Robert. He was staring off into the yard, ignoring them. As she turned back to Luke, he stretched closer to her and gave her a peck on the cheek. Maggie blushed, and Luke smiled.

"If you are done dawdling over there, Robert, let's get this house together before she gets it in her head to do it herself."

By late afternoon, everything was at least put away, and Maggie knew she could rearrange everything as she felt it necessary. The boxes were flattened and taken down to the trash barrel, and a cement block was dropped on top to hold them in place. Everyone was tired and dirty, so Luke headed for home, and the other two hit the showers. Robert fixed their supper, and they both wanted to turn in early. Maggie opted to take two of her prescription pain pills and headed to bed.

When Robert headed for home, he took a copy of the note their father had written to them. Maggie had found a small frame to put hers in and sat it on the table so she could read it every day. They both felt that their father was trying to tell them something, but he hadn't wanted anyone else to figure it out because of his paranoia. Luke planned to be back the following week to work on the house projects Maggie had been waiting to have fixed. He stopped to see her if he was in the neighborhood and checked on her healing progress or to just keep her company. Maggie always looked happy to see him, so Luke felt he was making progress.

The trial was coming up, and Maggie was becoming more nervous. Luke promised to sit with her whenever she was required to be in court. Robert offered to return, but Maggie told him it was nonsense as he wasn't required to be there. The lawyer said it was going to be an open-and-shut case against Gary, and the pictures law enforcement took of Maggie's injuries would get him much more jail time than the taking of her files and breaking into her house. Since he hadn't actually gotten his hand on the deed, there wasn't much they could charge him with on that count. But there were the other states just waiting to get their chance at trying him. A few days before the trial date, Gary Johnson pled guilty to everything and didn't fight extradition to any of the other states. He wrote a letter of apology to the Chesneys and agreed he needed help. The sheriff explained that Gary called his mother from jail, and she convinced him it was time to stop being a criminal and start being a man. The pastor from Gary's church also came to see him. Gary proceeded to write a check to the Kellers that not only covered what she had embezzled but an additional fifty thousand to pay off their house. It was the only way he felt he could make restitution for the damage he caused Maggie. He wrote a check to the Kellers' daughter, Jessie, as Gary had taken business from her, and she hadn't realized how he had used her to help fund his scams. Gary was going to be spending a long time in jail and had plenty of time to try to change his ways. Maggie had a hard time believing he had changed so quickly, and the next thing she knew, Gary was on his way to the state pen for her massive assault and would go from there to other states as the extraditions were applied.

Maggie looked in the mirror. The bruises on the outside were gone, but the scars inside were still there. She made an appointment with the pastor at New Hope Church for some counseling sessions. It was Luke's idea and one she should have thought of herself. She had gone through a lot that summer, and she needed to find closure. Luke's friendship was special, and she was depending on him being there. She smiled and saw the person that she used to see when she looked in the mirror. *I'll be alright in time.*

Luke arrived to spend a little time on Maggie's growing list of repairs. He started on the main floor and worked his way through the list. Most of the repairs were simple, and he encouraged Maggie to let him do them and allow herself to fully recover so she could get back to teaching. Maggie went to town one day as she had an appointment with the school to finish up the hiring process. Luke was down to the last few items on her list. He was working on the handrail to the basement and then would redo the treads. Several of them had cracks, and one was completely loose on the front. He had no idea how Maggie managed to not fall due to the disrepair.

Luke's father had a little lumber left from Maggie's trees, and Luke made all new stair treads and rails from them. He cut and stained them over at his father's before bringing them to the house. Since Maggie's arrival and Seth getting to know her, Luke and his father were getting along much better and could actually do small projects together. Seth had finally accepted the changes Luke had made to his life and agreed that Maggie was one special lady.

Luke had finished the new handrail and sat back on his heels. Next were the treads, and he decided to work from the bottom up. He wanted to get them done before Maggie returned from town.

He would rip one off and replace it. The stain was a deep mahogany, and as he continued to rip and replace, the whole staircase was turning from a disaster to something of beauty. When he got to the loose tread, he popped it off and noticed that attached to the inside stairwell was a key hanging on a nail. He reached over and picked up the key and proceeded to drop it. The noise it made when it landed sounded like it bounced off something metal. Luke went to the toolbox and got out a flashlight, looked down, and gasped. Luke worked on getting the next three treads torn off so he could get down inside and find the key.

Maggie returned home and found Luke sitting at the table with a key in his hands. "Hi, Maggie. How was your day?"

"Good. You want to help me bring a few groceries in? I plan on fixing us a nice supper tonight. You finish the stairway yet?"

Luke got up and left the key on the table. As they went back to the car, Luke said, "Not quite, but close. I need to replace one more tread."

They carried in the groceries, and Maggie put things away. Luke had sat back down at the kitchen table and picked up the key again. Maggie finally noticed. "What's the key for?"

"Sit down, Maggie." She sat down beside him. Luke pulled the framed letter from her father over beside her. "Read this again. Just the riddle. Out loud."

Maggie did and turned a puzzled look to Luke.

"What am I working on today?"

"The stairs."

"More specifically than the stairs."

Maggie thought for a bit. "The treads." Suddenly, Maggie looked as if a lightbulb had turned on. "The treads! Did you find something?"

"This key was hooked on a nail under that loose tread. The one that you had to be careful not to trip on when you came up the stairs."

Maggie jumped up and got the key ring that was found in the chest. "It matches the key on the ring. What does it go to?"

Luke reached over and took her hand and grabbed the flashlight he had left on the counter. "Come see the new handrail and treads. But be careful because I left that one off."

Maggie followed Luke and was surprised by how beautiful the new stairs were. "These are gorgeous! And they came from my trees! Oh, thank you so much, Luke!" She grabbed him and gave him a big hug.

"Let's go down the steps, but be careful of the one I haven't replaced yet."

Maggie followed him down and looked up at the stairs. "They are gorgeous. Wow."

Luke smiled. "Now come up to open one." He led Maggie up the stairs and had her sit on the tread below the open area, handed her the flashlight, and told her to turn it on and look inside. She did and had to blink several times to figure out what she was looking at.

Suddenly, Maggie looked at Luke. "Is that a strong box?"

"Yes, and let me show you something." He reached over and found the rope that was tied to the top of the box and hooked to the inside of the stairwell and pulled the box up. The box was heavy, and it barely fit through the opening, but Luke got it out and sat it on the step above them before removing the rope.

"What's in it?"

"I didn't open it, Maggie. That's your business. And now that I have it out of there, I'm going to either put in the tread permanently, or I can put a hinge on it for you to use again if you want."

"Hmmm. No. Put it on right. My dad had every reason to be paranoid, but everything is okay now."

"You take the box upstairs, and I'll finish the tread. You go on ahead and open it up."

Maggie picked up the heavy strong box and hauled it upstairs. She was glad that her muscles were back to normal and could lift without hurting. As she sat it on the kitchen table, she decided to clean the outside first. She used a damp cloth and cleaned the dust off and then sat the box on a towel so it wouldn't mar the table. She sat down in front of it and stared at the box. As bad as she wanted to open it, Maggie decided to call Robert instead.

Robert answered right away, and Maggie explained what Luke had found and how she wanted to open it with him on the phone. Robert was excited and happy that she had called him. "Open it up! See what that crazy dad of ours hid from us this time!"

Maggie laid the phone down, put it on speaker, reached over to pick up the key, and grabbed the lock. "Here goes nothing!" Maggie put the key in the lock and opened the lid.

Robert was impatient. "What do you see? What do you see?"

Maggie looked perplexed. "Nothing. There is a top tray and nothing in it."

"Take the tray out. You said the thing was heavy."

"I know. I guess I'm just a bit scared at finding nothing again."

"It's okay, Maggie. Just get it over with."

Maggie lifted the tray and found two bundles in paper bags. "Hmmm. There are two bags, and each one has our name on it."

Robert heard the rustle of paper as she lifted one out of the box. Luke had finished the step and stood watching Maggie. She smiled at him and then opened her bag. "Good Lord, Robert. We found the money!"

"What?"

"The bags are full of money. One for you and one for me."

"Good grief. Do I dare ask how much?"

Maggie was visibly shaking. "I don't know. A lot." Luke walked over and gave her a hug.

"Robert, I'll help Maggie count. She's shaking so bad I don't think she can do it. Do you want to wait, or shall we call you back?"

"I'll wait. Count out loud."

Luke counted and counted. Maggie sat and stared at the piles of money in front of her. The denominations were all one-hundred-dollar bills, and the amount kept adding up. Her brain froze, and she couldn't comprehend the amount. Luke could hear Robert gasp on the other end as he continued to count. When he finished, Luke said, "Robert, that is all from Maggie's bag. I assume there is the same amount in yours as they looked like the same size."

"Good grief. Dad was really paranoid."

Maggie finally shook herself and tried to take it all in. "Robert, I'll have Luke help me take this to the safety deposit box at the bank tomorrow. Once we get our act together, we can decide what to do with it. I can't leave it here like Dad did. I don't need the stress."

"Sounds like a plan. I just can't believe it. You're right. It's going to take some time to process. Thanks for finding it, Luke! I'll talk to you guys tomorrow. I can't wait to tell my wife!"

Luke looked at the money and then at Maggie. "Now you know what your dad was doing with all the money."

"I know. It's crazy. He claimed it on his taxes, but he never put it in the bank. It's. Just. Crazy."

Luke pulled Maggie into his arms. "I'm crazy for you." Luke reached down and placed a searing kiss on Maggie's lips, then cradled her in his arms. Maggie felt warm and safe. Safe. She hadn't felt that way for a long time. She looked up at Luke and kissed him back.

EPILOGUE

Their father had saved cash for several years, and both Luke and Maggie ended up being millionaires.

The wedding went off without a hitch. The couple had decided on a Christmas wedding, and for a honeymoon, they decided to go somewhere warm. Robert used some of his cash to pay for the honeymoon and sent them off in style.

Luke moved to the farm, and Maggie continued to teach part-time. They hoped to raise a large family and planned an addition to the house that would be started in the spring. Of course, Luke's father was going to be the contractor, and Luke planned to help, as long as he stayed out his father's way.

Robert finally came to understand the peacefulness of the farm that Maggie had enjoyed all her life. He planned on having a guest house built where the barn used to stand, and he and the family would be spending more time with Maggie and Luke. Seth had his hands full with all of the building projects the next year.

King had his own doghouse with built-in heating and air conditioning. He truly was king of his castle.

The estate auction went off as planned, and the money was donated to several food banks in the area.

Joe and Sheila became some of their best friends and got together frequently to celebrate birthdays and holidays. Maggie and Robert kept the rate for leasing their ground at a figure that benefited all. Mr. Beal had decided to retire the following year, and the couple wanted to move closer to their family. He offered to sell his small farm to Maggie and Robert; they agreed to the price and added another section of land to their holdings. Joe and Sheila offered to rent all of the additional land.

Mr. Jensen finally moved away once the sheriff decided there was nothing to hold him. No one ever heard from him again. The bank was able to survive and improve their reputation again. A local chain offered to buy it to add a branch, and the bank board decided it was time to let it go.

The Kellers found a job managing a local motel, and they could live on-site. They sold their house and moved into the motel. They took the money from the house and put it in savings. The money that Gary Johnson had given them went directly to pay the Chesneys back. They told their daughter, Jessie, she had to make her own way in the world. Jessie closed her realtor office and stayed home with her family.

The last Maggie heard about Gary Johnson, he would serve two years in the state pen for her assault and then be moved to Ohio for sentencing. Gary had saved a lot of money in several banks in every state he had run a con in and was diligently working on returning funds to everyone he stole it from. He had given his mother money also, but she left it in a separate account and refused to spend it. She would give it back to Gary after he was out of jail for the last time. Gary began counseling and spending time with the jail pastor. It was difficult to admit how wrong he had been and how greed had taken over. It was actually a relief to no longer look over his shoulder.

Maggie had an occasional nightmare and still couldn't sit down at the pond alone, but as long as Luke was with her, she felt safe.

The shotgun had been locked away, and Maggie hoped she never needed it again. Luke would still find her sitting under the elm tree daydreaming, King by her side, and he would join her frequently to enjoy the peace and quiet.

Luke kept busy with his repair business. He and his father had become close again, and Seth accepted Luke would not return to his home church. Seth and his whole family loved Maggie and Robert and were happy to be their neighbors.

The Following Spring

Maggie and Luke stood by the pond and watched ducks with little ones floating on the nearly overflowing water. Luke had kept the grasses cut surrounding the area to be able to watch for snakes. Maggie still refused to come by herself, but Luke was happy to join her in a walk almost every night. Maggie was just beginning to show, and Luke was excited to become a father. Seth had started on the addition, and it would be completed in time for their new arrival. Once the addition was done, Seth would start on the guest house for Robert. Maggie turned to Luke and lovingly touched his cheek. "I couldn't ask for more."

ABOUT THE AUTHOR

Diane is from Southwest Nebraska and was raised on a farm in the area. As she wrote this story, she used fond memories of friends and family. It is fictional, but the friendships and ideas that neighbors helping neighbors has always been a large part of the farming community.

Fic Win
Winters, Diane,
Dangerous inheritance

CPSIA information can be obtained
at www.ICGtesting.com
Printed in the USA
FFOW03n1813180617
36751FF